Chris betrayed no emotion. After a moment he said, "What are the conditions?"

"I want a whole new wardrobe."

His mouth quirked a little. "Of course."

"And I want a thousand pounds when—when you grow tired of me."

Something flickered in his eyes, but he said, "All right."

Still watching her, he said on an odd note, "And just what do I get in return for all this?"

Tiffany looked at him and swallowed. "I'll—I'll be anything you want me to be."

Dear Reader,

The wild and primitive scenery of the Douro valley.
The white baroque palaces. What men would live and
rule here? Calum came first, a tall and golden god,
but then Francesca pushed her way into my mind.
Then Chris, very much a man of the world. A family,
then—outwardly tamed, but with hidden emotions as
deep and hot-blooded as the land they lived in. Three
cousins who filled my imagination, fascinating,
absorbing, clamoring to come alive. And three wishes
that had to come true. Then I thought of an
anniversary, and saw a girl, sitting entirely alone on
the riverbank....

Sally Wentworth

Books by Sally Wentworth

HARLEQUIN PRESENTS

Don't miss any of our special offers. Write to us at the
following address for information on our newest releases.

Harlequin Reader Service
U.S.: 3010 Walden Ave., P.O. Box 1325, Buffalo, NY 14269
Canadian: P.O. Box 609, Fort Erie, Ont. L2A 5X3

SALLY WENTWORTH

Chris

Harlequin Books

TORONTO • NEW YORK • LONDON
AMSTERDAM • PARIS • SYDNEY • HAMBURG
STOCKHOLM • ATHENS • TOKYO • MILAN
MADRID • WARSAW • BUDAPEST • AUCKLAND

ISBN 0-373-11832-5

CHRIS

First North American Publication 1996.

Copyright © 1995 by Sally Wentworth.

PROLOGUE

BRODEY HOUSE BICENTENNIAL

The magnificent eighteenth-century baroque palace of the Brodey family, situated on the banks of the River Douro in Portugal, will soon be *en fête* for a whole week to celebrate the two hundredth anniversary of their company.

The House of Brodey, famous the world over for its fine wines, especially port and Madeira, has now diversified into many other commodities and is one of the biggest family-owned companies in Europe. Originally founded in the beautiful island of Madeira, the company spread to Oporto when Calum Lennox Brodey the first went there two centuries ago to purchase thousands of acres of land in the picturesque Douro valley. That land is now covered with the millions of grape-vines that produce the port on which the family fortune is based.

A FAMILY AFFAIR

Just like any family, every member of the Brodey clan will be in Oporto to welcome their guests from all over the world to the festivities.

Patriarch of the family, Calum Lennox Brodey, named after his ancestor, as are all the eldest sons in the main line, is reported to be greatly looking forward not only to the celebrations but also to the family reunion. Old Calum, as he's popularly known in wine-growing circles, is in his eighties now but still takes a keen interest in the wine-producing side of the company, and is often to be seen by his admiring workers strolling among the vines to check on the crop or tasting the vintage in the family's bottling plant near Oporto.

STILL HAUNTED BY THE PAST

Although the anniversary will be a happy one, in the past there has been terrible tragedy within the family. Some twenty-two years ago Old Calum's two eldest sons and their wives were involved in a fatal car-smash while on holiday in Spain, all four being killed. Each couple had a son of roughly the same age and Old Calum bravely overcame his grief as he took the boys into his palace and brought them up himself, both of them eventually following in his footsteps by joining the company.

It was rumoured at the time of this overwhelmingly tragic accident that old Mr Brodey looked to his third son, Paul, to help run the business. Paul Brodey, however, was hooked on painting and is now a celebrated artist. He lives near Lisbon with his wife Maria, who is half Portuguese and is herself a well-known painter. The good news is, though, that their only child, Christopher, has joined the family firm on the sales side and is based mainly in New York.

Only one of Old Calum's grandsons now shares the splendour of the palace, which is mainly decorated in Renaissance style, with him. This is the only child of his late eldest son, who, following the family tradition, is also called Calum—Young Calum, in this case. The younger Calum Brodey, around thirty years old and one of the most eligible bachelors in the country, if not in Europe, has virtually taken over the running of the company, but will be gracefully taking a back seat to his grandfather during the week's festivities.

MARRIAGE IN MIND?

Another extraordinary tradition peculiar to the family is that all the men maintain their links with their mother country by marrying blonde English girls. Every son of the family for the past several generations has travelled to the UK and returned with a beautiful 'English rose' on his arm. Will Young Calum and Christopher carry on the tradition, we wonder?

The third Brodey grandson, Lennox, who now lives in Madeira with his beautiful and adored wife Stella, who is expecting their first child later this year, will be among the family guests. Stella, of course, is a blonde and lovely English girl.

Old Calum's fourth child, his elegant daughter Adele, is married to the well-known French millionaire, the gallant and still handsome Guy de Charenton, an assiduous worker for the Paris Opera and for the many charities that he supports.

Although the Brodey family has many connections with the upper echelons of society, especially in England, it was Adele's daughter and only child, the sensationally beautiful Francesca, who finally linked it to the aristocracy with her marriage to Prince Paolo de Vieira a few years ago. This marriage, which took place in the Prince's fairy-tale castle in Italy, looked all set to have the proverbial happy ending, but, alas, this wasn't to be and the couple parted after only two years. Since then Francesca's name has been linked with several men, including lately Michel, the Comte de la Fontaine, seen with her on her many shopping trips in Paris and Rome.

To all the glamorous members of the Brodey family we extend our warm congratulations on their anniversary, and we are sure that all their lucky guests will have the most lavish and memorable time at the bicentennial celebrations.

THE HOUSE OF BRODEY

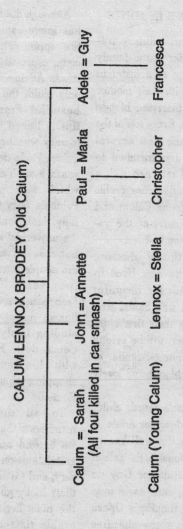

CALUM LENNOX BRODEY (Old Calum)

```
        ┌───────────────────┬──────────────────┬──────────────────┐
Calum = Sarah         John = Annette      Paul = Maria      Adele = Guy
(All four killed in car smash)
        │                    │                 │                  │
Calum (Young Calum)   Lennox = Stella    Christopher        Francesca
```

CHAPTER ONE

THEY were all there—the Brodeys—gathered together in the beautiful gardens of their magnificent baroque *palácio* near Oporto. All of them had come to celebrate the two hundredth anniversary of the House of Brodey.

This lunch party was the first in a week of festivities that would culminate in a grand ball, but today there were only about a hundred and fifty invited guests—and one gatecrasher.

Those guests who had received official invitations were mostly in the wine trade: buyers from France, America, Britain, even as far away as Australia; local shippers; expert viniculturists from the Brodey bottling plant in Vila Nova de Gaia and from their many *quintas* in the Alto Douro. There was a preponderance of men in dark suits, the women mostly wives or daughters invited out of courtesy.

The members of the family moved easily among them, working their way through the guests, their presence marked by the eddying circles of people around them. Perhaps the largest group was gathered around the head of the house, Calum Lennox Brodey; Old Calum, they called him, in his eighties now and his tall back a little stooped, but his eyes still bright with intelligence and enjoyment of life as he talked and laughed with his guests. A group of almost equal size stood near his grandson and heir, also named Calum, who ran the family business—or perhaps empire would be a better name for it, so wide were its interests now.

A girl—a tall, slender blonde in a flamboyantly coloured outfit that stood out from the dark business suits like a flame tree—broke away from one of the groups and went to take a glass of iced white port from one of the waiters. She was followed by a man in his late thirties, equally tall, with lean features and figure, and an air of suave charm that could only denote a Frenchman. He said something to the girl and put a possessive hand on her shoulder, but she shook him off and went to talk to some guests who were looking a little lost, smiling with warmth and putting them immediately at ease. Her name was Princess Francesca de Vieira and she was Old Calum Brodey's granddaughter, and the man with her was a French count, rumoured to be her next husband.

There were also other members of the family from the Madeiran branch of the company at the party, but it was these three—Old Calum and his two grandchildren—that held the fixed attention of Tiffany Dean as she stood just inside one of the stone archways that led on to the terrace above the rich green lawns on which the guests stood. She knew so much about the Brodeys, had been studying them for the past two weeks, ever since she'd determined to gatecrash this party. There had been plenty of information about them, in the local Portuguese papers, of course, and in international magazines; Francesca especially had figured in the latter, her spectacular marriage to an Italian prince and her even more spectacular divorce having been grist to the mill for the gossip columnists and the even busier paparazzi.

Tiffany watched her, envious of the bright trouser-suit and even more so of the other girl's obviously innate air of self-confidence that could only come from never having to worry about money, from always having the best of everything. The best education, the best clothes—even the best men.

The younger Calum Brodey carried himself the same way, with the same slightly arrogant tilt to the chin that would have singled him out from the crowd even if he hadn't been so tall and fair-haired. All the Brodeys were fair because it was a tradition among them that they always married blonde women—their 'English roses', as some romantically minded journalist had called them in an article Tiffany had read as part of her research into the family. Although she'd had no training, she had herself written a couple of articles for a magazine—light, female-orientated pieces—and her contact there, realising that an Englishwoman might stand more chance than a local, had asked her to try and do an inside story on the Brodeys, especially young Calum.

Ordinarily Tiffany would have refused—such an invasion of privacy wasn't her scene—but circumstances had forced her to accept. The first reason was of course her almost complete lack of money; she had been out of a job for so long that she was already on the breadline and fast becoming desperate. The second was more personal. She remembered her contact, a junior editor, coming to see her and offering what seemed like a huge sum if she could get close to Calum, dig up some new gossip. 'With your looks and your blonde hair,' the man had said persuasively, 'it will be easy for you. Just try to find out what goes on behind the public face they all show to the world. There's no harm in it; they're used to publicity and love it even if they say they don't.'

Tiffany was shrewd enough to know that that probably wasn't true, and despite her poverty would have refused the assignment. But she had a grudge against the Brodeys. It was through them that she'd lost the job that had brought her to Portugal in the first place. Not that

she'd ever come even close to meeting any of them, of
course; she had been a very insignificant cog in the large
business project of which the Brodey Corporation was
the principal financial investor. And it had been the
Brodeys who had been the first to back out when the
recession hit, making the other investors follow suit so
that the project collapsed, leaving herself and all the
other workers out of a job. It was her seething resentment at this uncaring ruthlessness that had finally
overcome her scruples and misgivings and made her
accept the on-results-only assignment. So she had gatecrashed the party, knowing it was her last chance. Her
last desperate throw of the dice.

It had been far easier to get into the *palácio* than she'd
dared to hope; Tiffany had waited until there was a queue
of cars at the gate and people had started to get out
impatiently and walk down the driveway, then she had
merely joined a small group and walked in with them,
not even needing the sentence about joining her husband
inside that she had carefully rehearsed in Portuguese in
case she was asked to show her invitation. But now that
she was here she had to think of a way of getting herself
introduced to Calum Brodey, hopefully in a way that
would attract his attention. Once he'd noticed her all she
had to do was hold his attention long enough for him
to get interested in her. If her luck changed. If he even
bothered to look at her.

Biting her lip, Tiffany determined to be positive.
Taking a deep breath, she walked down the terrace steps
to join the party.

A waiter came around the side of the house carrying
a tray of filled glasses. Seeing Tiffany without a drink,
he paused so that she could take a glass. As she did so
another hand, male, reached out from behind her to take
one. Glancing over her shoulder, she saw a tall, broad-

shouldered man in a light-coloured suit. She went to walk on, but he said, 'Hi, there. You look as if you might speak English.'

His accent immediately identified him as North American, from the States probably.

Tiffany hesitated a moment, then nodded. 'Do you have some kind of problem?'

'Only that I don't speak Portuguese and I hardly know anyone here. I saw you standing over there, watching everyone, and figured you might be in the same boat.' He held out his free hand and gave her an engaging grin. 'The name's Sam, Sam Gallagher.'

Again Tiffany hesitated; she didn't want to get stuck with the American, but on the other hand it might be useful to have a man in tow for a while. So she smiled in return and shook his hand. 'I'm Tiffany Dean.'

He gave her an appreciative glance, his eyes running over her slim, petite figure in the silk suit it had cost her last penny to hire, and coming back to her face. Amusement came into his eyes as he saw that she raised a cool eyebrow, but he merely looked at his glass suspiciously and said, 'What is this stuff?'

'Don't you know? It's white port. The "in" aperitif all over Europe. I wouldn't know about the States. Is that where you're from?'

'How'd you guess? Yeah, I'm from Wyoming.'

'Do they drink a lot of port there? Are you a vintner?'

'A wine-seller? Hell, no.'

'I thought everyone at this party was connected with the wine trade in some way,' Tiffany remarked. But she was making small talk, her eyes going past Sam, searching the crowd for Calum Brodey. She saw him momentarily, crossing the lawn to speak to a red-haired woman who seemed to be connected with the caterers. After the woman had nodded and hurried away, he turned back to mingle again. Tiffany began to move in his direction.

Sam, following her, said, 'No, I have a friend who works over here with a shipping company. He couldn't make it today so he gave me the invite. It's quite some party. Much bigger than I expected. Do you know these Brodeys?'

She gave a casual shrug. 'Everyone does. They're one of the leading families in Oporto. That's the head of the family, over there.' She gestured towards old Mr Brodey. 'He's talking to one of his grandsons, Lennox Brodey, and his wife—the blonde, pregnant woman,' she pointed.

Looking at the couple, Tiffany felt a surge of wistful jealousy. They looked so happy together, were obviously deeply in love, the woman radiant in her pregnancy, the man openly solicitous for her welfare. Two of the lucky ones, not forever being knocked down by malignant fate until one was too punch-drunk to dare to hope any more.

She nodded to where Francesca de Vieira stood among a small crowd of attentive men. 'That's his granddaughter, in the flame-coloured outfit.'

Sam followed her glance and she heard his sharp intake of breath. But that, she thought with some chagrin, was the kind of effect the other girl would always have on men. Drawing herself up, Tiffany fervently wished she were a foot taller, but then laughed rather scornfully at herself; no way was she ever going to grow so she had just better make the most of what she'd got. And her best assets, she knew, were her thick bell of blonde hair and a pair of large, long-lashed blue eyes set above a cute turned-up nose and a wide mouth. Not a beautiful face, but one that made people look twice, especially when she smiled or laughed, her whole face lighting up.

Her figure, though unfashionably short in her own eyes, was also good enough to merit a second glance.

'Do you live here in Portugal?' Sam asked her as they walked on again.

'Temporarily,' Tiffany replied, in a tone that didn't encourage him to go on. 'I know hardly anyone here so I'm afraid I can't introduce you.'

It was meant to put him off, to stop him asking more questions, to encourage him to go and find someone else, but Sam said, 'No more do I, so I guess we may as well stick with each other.'

They were in the centre of the throng of guests now, and Tiffany would rather have been on her own. If Sam had known people, could have introduced her around, it would have been different, but she certainly didn't want him at her side the whole afternoon. Finishing her drink, she handed him the glass and said with a smile, 'It's so hot; do you think you could find me another one of these? But with plenty of ice, please,' she added so that it would take him longer.

'Sure thing. Don't go away; I'll be right back.'

He moved towards the edge of the crowd, looking for a waiter. As soon as he was hidden from sight, Tiffany walked quickly to the part of the garden where she'd seen Calum Brodey. As she did so another group, consisting wholly of men, broke up amid a burst of laughter. One man turned away, a grin still on his face, and bumped into Tiffany.

'*Perdao*!' the man exclaimed, putting out a hand to steady her.

'Er... *Não tem de que.*'

He laughed. 'You're obviously not Portuguese.'

'Oh, dear. Was it that bad?' Tiffany smiled, her eyes lighting up.

'Ten out of ten for effort.'

'But not for pronunciation, I take it?' Tiffany said ruefully. She glanced at his good-looking features under longish brown hair, thinking that his face seemed vaguely familiar. 'But you don't sound Portuguese either.'

'I'm bilingual,' he admitted. 'Comes of having a mother who's half Portuguese herself.' Holding out his hand, he said, 'I'm Christopher Brodey.'

Of course! That was where she'd seen his face before: in the articles that she'd studied. But as he wasn't in the direct family line Tiffany hadn't taken much notice of him. She tried to recall what she'd read and remembered that he had a reputation for being pretty wild in his youth. And he was still young, in his late twenties, she guessed, so maybe he still went in for fast cars, fast boats and fast women. But he might be useful.

So Tiffany shook his hand and gave him one of her best smiles as she told him her name.

'Tiffany. That's pretty. And unusual.' His eyes went over her and he gave her the kind of smile that let her know he found her pretty and unusual, too. 'I'm sure we haven't met before or I'd have remembered. But then, I'm not often in Portugal nowadays.' She raised a questioning eyebrow and he explained, 'It's my job to open up new markets for our wine, so I travel a lot.'

'Really? That sounds exciting. And from what I've heard you must be a great salesman,' she said flatteringly. 'You sell all over the world now, don't you?'

'Not quite.' He shrugged that off with a grin. 'But I get around.'

He had an attractive smile, all crinkly eyes and boyishness. It wasn't difficult to see how he'd got his reputation, with women anyway.

'Where are you actually based?' she asked.

'That's a difficult question. My parents live in Lisbon and have a villa in Madeira, where I lived while I was learning the wine trade. But now I spend most of my time in New York because the American market is really taking off.'

'Oporto must be quite a come-down, then,' Tiffany remarked, her interest caught.

Chris shook his head. 'No, I like New York, but Portugal is home.' Turning, he nodded towards the house. 'And this is where I live when I'm here—with my grandfather and my cousin.'

Turning with him, Tiffany lifted her head to look at the *palácio*. It was so ornate, so beautiful. Two deep wings stood on either side of a magnificent entrance topped by the Brodey coat of arms, reached by fairy-tale staircases that branched on both sides. The walls were stark white but were relieved by the many windows topped with ornate stone pediments. There were statues on the gable-ends and huge pepper-pot chimneys on the roof, and next to the left wing a chapel that looked too delicate to hold the mass of columns and baroque stonework that covered it. And everything was so beautifully maintained, the gravel free of weeds, the box hedges of the parterres clipped to uniformity, the cherubs on the fountain in the lake sparkling in the sunlight.

'It's quite a place,' Tiffany said unsteadily, then added quickly, in case he guessed that she was overawed, 'But a perfect setting to celebrate a bicentennial, of course. Is yours the oldest port company in the area?' she asked, already knowing the answer but wanting to keep him talking.

'No, there are others that are much older. We're comparative newcomers. But you haven't got a drink.' He looked round, saw a waiter, clicked his fingers, and the man immediately came over. Chris took one too, and sipped it as he said, 'How come you got invited to the party?'

'Ah, well...' Tiffany gave him a mischievous smile and put a delicately fingered hand on his sleeve as she leaned nearer to him. 'You promise you won't give me away?'

An amused look came into Chris's grey eyes. 'I'm renowned for my discretion.'

Tiffany didn't believe that for a minute, but she said confidingly, 'I wasn't really invited. A colleague couldn't come and passed on the invitation,' she told him, borrowing Sam Gallagher's excuse. 'And as I hardly know anyone in Oporto I thought it would be nice to come along and perhaps meet some people who speak English.' She smiled up at him. 'And you see, it worked; I've met you for a start.'

'Well, I'm very glad you came. And where do you work in Oporto?'

'Down in the commercial district,' Tiffany said airily, adding quickly, 'I suppose you know everyone here. Will you introduce me to a few people who speak English? Your family, perhaps?'

Chris's mouth twisted a little wryly, as if he saw through her, but he said, 'Of course. Now, let's see who's near.' He looked round. Tall, but not exceptionally so, he was still able to see over the heads of the many Portuguese guests. 'Ah, yes,' he said. 'This way.' And, putting a hand under her elbow, he led her through the throng.

Tapping a shoulder, murmuring, '*Com licença*,' he came up to where his cousin stood. But it was the wrong cousin. He'd brought her to Francesca de Vieira, and Tiffany was angrily certain that he had done so deliberately. But even the wrong cousin was better than no cousin at all, Tiffany supposed, so she smiled as the two were introduced and looked at the other girl admiringly.

'You're so lucky to be tall, Princess.'

'Please, call me Francesca. And I don't consider it an advantage. Think what a choice of men you have compared to me.'

They both laughed and looked each other over. Tiffany guessed that they were about the same age—twenty-five—and they were both blonde, but there the similarity ended. Francesca was the willowy type, thin as a reed, and able to carry off expensive designer clothes with the elegance of a trained model. Her long hair was gathered on the top of her head in a style that looked casual with loose strands framing her face, but must have taken a hairdresser an hour to do. She wore chunky costume jewellery round her neck and wrists, along with some breathtaking rings that could only be real. She'd married one rich, aristocratic husband and had another lined up. She was sleek and pampered and, on top of everything else, beautiful.

With the great disadvantage of being short, Tiffany on the other hand had to be careful to wear clothes of soft shades, like the grey silk suit she'd hired for today; bright, jazzy colours made her look ridiculous. The same went for her hair; it had to be smooth and fairly short otherwise it looked plain untidy. And if she hadn't already sold what jewellery she had, she could never have worn anything that wasn't simple and small. And as for men—well, that was about par for the course where her life was concerned.

As Tiffany looked at Francesca she knew she ought to hate her, but she was disarmed by the rich girl's warmth and friendliness.

'Tiffany doesn't speak Portuguese very well and doesn't know anyone here,' Chris explained. 'So I've taken her under my wing.'

His cousin flicked him an amused, speculative look. 'Didn't you bring her?'

Chris returned the look, then glanced at the Count. 'No, I hadn't anyone I cared to invite. We met quite by chance.'

'How fortunate for you,' Francesca said with irony.

Tiffany realised they were sparring with one another, that they knew each other well enough to tease about their private lives. Francesca's French Count realised it too, because he put a possessive hand on her arm.

'The buffet is about to be served. Where do you wish to sit?'

He spoke in French and Francesca answered him in the same language. 'If you're hungry, then go and eat. I'll come when I'm ready.'

And there, Tiffany thought sardonically, lies the greatest difference between us. She can dismiss a man, who obviously dotes on her, almost rudely, while I must scheme and flatter just to try to get an introduction to a man who might not even like me.

But it acted as a further goad, and Tiffany put herself out to be as warm and vivacious as Francesca, making conversation with them for the next ten minutes or so as if she were used to moving in such élite circles, being as witty as she knew how, and letting her personality make up for the inequalities between them. She told a couple of anecdotes in a droll way that made Chris and Francesca laugh in genuine amusement, Chris's deep, masculine tones drawing the attention of several people around them. Tiffany hoped it would draw his other cousin over, because the lawn was starting to clear now as the guests moved towards the other side of the house where tables had been set out for lunch.

The Count had waited for Francesca despite her rebuff, but now she took pity on him. 'I suppose we'd better go and eat. Tiffany, you will come and sit with us, won't you?' She looked round. 'Now, where's Calum?'

Thanking her stars that things seemed to be going right at last, Tiffany smiled an acceptance of the invitation and began to stroll along with them. Calum Brodey glanced round from the group he was with and crossed to join them. His eyes flicked to Tiffany, but then he looked at Francesca and said, 'Remember Grandfather wants us to split up.'

Francesca pouted. 'Do we have to? I haven't seen you or Chris for simply ages. I'd much rather sit with you both.'

Calum gave her an indulgent look. 'We can catch up on all our news over dinner tonight.'

'But Grandfather will be there, and you can't *really* talk when he's listening. The dear old darling gets so upset sometimes if you tell the truth, the whole truth and nothing but the truth. Not to mention the parents,' she added with feeling.

'You shouldn't lead such a wild life,' Calum told her, but he was smiling as he said it, just as everyone seemed to smile at Francesca.

'All right, we'll split up.' Turning towards Tiffany, Francesca said, 'I'm so sorry, Tiffany. Now you'll have to put up with Chris. How boring for you.'

'Hey!' Chris protested in an injured tone.

Calum laughed and looked at Tiffany. 'I don't think we've met.'

Tiffany gave a great sigh of relief and pleasure and prepared to be devastating. But just at that moment Sam Gallagher strolled up to them.

'Tiffany! So there you are. I'm afraid the ice in your drink melted so I drank it myself.' He looked round the group, all of them regarding him with different expressions, and said a genial, 'Hi there.'

If Tiffany had been capable of mental annihilation he would have disappeared into dust. Couldn't the stupid man see that he wasn't wanted, for heaven's sake? But he just stood there, grinning amiably, expecting her to welcome him back. She sensed Calum's withdrawal and said quickly, desperately trying to retrieve the situation, 'This is Mr—er—I'm sorry, I can't remember your name. One of your other guests,' she said to Calum, with a look that disowned Sam entirely.

'It's Gallagher. Sam Gallagher.' Sam held out his hand to Calum and Chris, then to Francesca. 'I guess you must be the Princess.'

'I guess I must be, at that,' Francesca agreed, giving him an amused, mischievous look. 'Have you been looking for Tiffany?'

'Yeah. I went to get her a drink but she kind of disappeared. Found someone else to talk to, I guess.'

Chris gave Tiffany a wry smile. 'Sorry, I didn't intend to tread on anyone's toes.'

Still fighting valiantly, Tiffany gave him a sparkling smile and said, referring to the way he'd bumped into her, 'The only toes you—nearly—trod on were mine.'

But it wasn't enough. He smiled in appreciation of her wit, but clapped Calum on the shoulder and said, 'OK, if we have to split up, let's go.' And the two cousins walked off together.

If there had been a cliff handy Tiffany would have thrown herself over it. Just why was it, she wondered bitterly, that everything always went wrong for her? Just what had she done to make some cruel fate decree that every time she took one step forward she could guarantee to be knocked back to the end of the street? And just why had that same fate provided a man as thick-headed as Sam Gallagher to cross her path today of all days?

Tiffany was good at hiding her feelings, knowing that all people wanted to see was a pretty, animated face. People had enough problems of their own without being bothered by those of a total stranger. She tried to hide them as she realised that there was nothing now to stay for; she might as well leave.

But perhaps Francesca noticed, because after looking at her she said, 'But *we* don't have to split up. Come and sit with Michel and me, Tiffany. And you too, of course, Mr Gallagher.'

'Sure thing.' Sam put a hand on Tiffany's arm and began to walk along with them.

She shook him off, much as Francesca had shaken off the Count earlier, and gave him a look of cold dislike. But Sam seemed immune to that too, merely giving her a lazy grin as he strode along, making her have to hurry to keep up.

Tiffany felt dwarfed by the three of them and was glad when they found one of the large circular tables with some spare seats. But there were other people already there so she and Sam had to sit on the opposite side to Francesca and Michel. As the last guests came into the garden to take their seats, she saw that the caterer, watched by Calum, was hastily ordering a waiter to lay an extra place at another table. So now the Brodeys would know that they had an uninvited guest. Just great!

A trio was playing in the background, the food on the buffet was out of this world, but all Tiffany could hear was Calum's voice asking Chris to introduce her, and all she could taste was chagrin at the way Sam had butted in before he could do so.

The table was too wide to talk across it to Francesca; the man on Tiffany's other side was Portuguese and his English wasn't very good. Sam chatted to her, but she was so angry with him that at first she didn't answer. He glanced at her from long-lashed brown eyes, then concentrated on his food. As to be expected at a party given by a wine company, there were three wine glasses and a champagne flute in front of each guest. Waiters came to fill them with each course but it took a couple of glasses before Tiffany's bitterness melted away and she thought, What the hell? Tomorrow can go hang, just like all the other tomorrows that have come and gone. I'm here so I might as well make the best of it.

Turning to Sam, she said, 'Sorry.'

'Did I mess something up?'

She gave a wry laugh. 'Not really.' Then she sighed. 'No, there was nothing to mess up.' She smiled at him. 'Why don't you tell me about America?'

'America is a big country to talk about. Have you ever been there?'

'A couple of times, when I was a young child, to Disneyland for holidays. But I haven't been to—where did you say you came from? Wyoming, wasn't it?'

'That's right.'

'Isn't that cowboy country?'

'I guess you could call it that. There are certainly a lot of cattle ranges there.'

He began to tell her about it and she listened, at first politely, but then with growing interest. Sam had a way with words, could use them to paint a picture in her mind. He was amusing, too, so that for a while she forgot her troubles and lived in his world, which seemed infinitely preferable to her own. But then, few were not. She laughed at Sam's description of a rodeo he had attended once and, feeling herself watched, glanced across the table. The Count and the other man beside Francesca were both momentarily occupied by the people on their other sides. She had her eyes fixed on Tiffany and Sam, her head slightly tilted as she contemplated them and listened to Sam's deep tones. When Tiffany looked at her Francesca raised a suggestive eyebrow towards Sam, the question clear.

Tiffany shook her head the slightest fraction, letting her know she wasn't interested. Although she could have been, could have really enjoyed Sam's company, if he hadn't shot her ploy to pieces. Even though he was good-looking and a pleasant lunch companion, she didn't think she'd ever forgive him for that. It had meant so much—this last, desperate chance to earn some money.

Lunch came to an end; people began to get to their feet, to talk in clusters again for a while as they drank a last glass of port, deep amber-coloured this time, then drift towards one or another of their hosts to say goodbye before leaving. A feeling of fatalism stole over Tiffany: she had absolutely no idea how she was going to get out of the mess she was in. She had given it her best shot but it hadn't worked, thanks to Sam. Excusing herself, she went in search of the ladies' room, and found that a downstairs cloakroom in the house had been set aside for the purpose. Even the cloakroom took her breath away. There were beautifully draped curtains at the window, ornamental French hand-basins with gold taps, a dozen bottles of good perfume and hand lotion for the guests' use. How the other half lived, Tiffany thought with irony, remembering the shabby, antiquated bathroom she had to share with a dozen others, and that covertly. By nature fastidious, she thought that that was perhaps the most difficult thing to bear.

She washed her hands and applied fresh lipstick, helped herself to a liberal application of perfume and went out, down the long, cool, blue-tiled corridor, into the sun again. The brilliant light dazzled her, so Tiffany stood for a moment in the doorway, letting her eyes adjust. She made an unknowingly attractive picture, framed by an arch of deep yellow roses that climbed the wall, and drew the eyes of several people still in the garden. Francesca was there, holding on to her cousin

Chris's arm, almost as tall as he, and laughing at something he'd said. And Calum Brodey was overseeing the distribution of glasses of vintage port, mainly to the male guests. He had just given a glass to Sam, who saw Tiffany and walked to meet her as she came into the garden.

Sam smiled, then got a whiff of her perfume. He leaned nearer, his nose close to the delicate column of her neck, and murmured, 'Hey, you smell terrific.'

In that instant an idea leapt into Tiffany's mind. There was no time to think about whether it was right or what the outcome might be. It was a chance and she immediately took it.

Raising her hand, she gave Sam a hard, loud slap across the face. He jerked in surprise, the hand holding his glass coming up in automatic defence, the contents flying out. But he had no chance to say anything because Tiffany exclaimed in well-simulated anger, 'How dare you? You can take your disgusting suggestion and—and just go jump in that lake!' she cried out, and pointed dramatically.

As she'd hoped, everyone within earshot turned to look. For a moment there was a stunned silence, then everyone seemed to move and speak at once.

Sam exclaimed, 'What the hell...?' but she ran a few steps away from him, in the direction of Calum who had started towards her.

He strode up to Sam, got between him and Tiffany, and said in a voice that was colder than ice, 'My cousin will escort you to the gate.' And he beckoned Chris over.

'Now just a minute here, I——' Sam began angrily.

But Chris put a hand under his elbow. 'It's this way.'

Sam was bigger than he was, in both height and breadth, and could probably have pushed Chris away, but he looked across at Tiffany, who was standing near Calum. For a second their eyes met and he must have realised what game she was playing. He hesitated, then, seeing the tense pleading in her blue eyes, he gave an angry, resigned kind of shrug and let Chris lead him away.

Francesca watched them go, a frown between her eyes, then came over to Tiffany. 'Perhaps you'd better come inside with me.'

'Thank you, but if I could just wait a while until he's gone,' Tiffany said in a distressed voice.

'But your suit,' Francesca said, pointing.

Tiffany looked down and saw that Sam's port had spilled all down her. She gave a genuine wail of anguish. 'Oh, no!'

'Come into the house. I'm sure we can save it if we do something quickly.'

Calum added his voice. 'Yes, please go inside, Miss— er——?'

'Tiffany Dean,' Tiffany said abstractedly, still looking down at her skirt and wondering how on earth she was going to explain this to the shop she'd hired it from.

Francesca led her inside the house again and up to a bedroom where Tiffany slipped out of the suit and it was rushed away by a maid, who pulled a pessimistic face when she saw the stained silk. There was a towelling robe hanging in the next-door bathroom. Bringing it for her to put on, Francesca said, 'Will you excuse me, Tiffany? I must go and help say goodbye to the guests. I'll be back as soon as I can.'

'Yes, of course. I'm sorry to be a nuisance.'

'Nonsense. It wasn't your fault.'

Francesca smiled and hurried away, leaving Tiffany to realise that she'd got the introduction to Calum she'd so much wanted, but had had no opportunity to follow it up. It had all been wasted. She'd used poor Sam for nothing. It was a desperate ploy that had seemed a good

idea at the time, but just hadn't worked. The way most
of the ideas she had nowadays never seemed to work
out. And if the suit was ruined, then she was even worse
off than when she'd started.

That didn't bear thinking about so Tiffany resolutely
pushed it out of her mind. She caught a glimpse of herself
in a full-length antique mirror. The robe was much too
big, completely hiding her hands and falling to her feet,
looking ridiculous with her high heels. She kicked off
her shoes, feeling a mad urge to break into hysterical
laughter. It was that or cry. Pulling the robe round her,
she sat on the edge of the four-poster bed and fought
back tears. Please, please, she thought fiercely, let
something go right for a change. Just for once let it go
right.

There was a knock on the door and Francesca came
in. 'The guests have all left and my grandfather has gone
up to his room to rest.' She hesitated for a moment, then
said, 'We haven't told him what happened. We didn't
want to upset him. He hasn't been very well recently,
you see.'

'Oh, I'm sorry. He looks all right,' Tiffany remarked.

'Oh, yes. It's his blood-pressure. Arranging all these
festivities for the bicentennial has been a bit much for
him. Calum has tried to take as much of the organis-
ation on himself as he can, but Grandpa has insisted on
knowing every detail. It would be a shame if this—incident spoilt things for him on the first day.'

'I'm very sorry,' Tiffany said, guilt making her voice
stiff.

Francesca mistook the nuance in her voice and sat
down on the bed beside her. 'Oh, dear, I didn't mean it
that way. I'm so sorry, Tiffany. You must be feeling
wretched about it yourself. The stupid man! Why don't
they ever learn? You only have to smile at them and be

friendly and they immediately think you're willing to leap into bed with them. And Sam seemed OK, too. Just shows you how mistaken you can be.'

Tiffany could only manage a stilted smile at that, and quickly changed the subject. 'I don't know how I'm going to get home. Would it be OK to wait here until my suit's dry?'

'Of course. But you can't possibly spend the whole of the afternoon in here.' Francesca laughed. 'I'd lend you something of mine, but you'd be swamped in it. But I'll see what I can arrange.' She stood up. 'Calum wants to speak to you. He's downstairs.' And she headed for the door.

Tiffany stared at her. 'What about?'

The taller girl shrugged, laughed. 'He didn't tell me. He never does. Come and see.'

Tiffany got uncertainly to her feet and gestured to the bathrobe. 'Like this? I can't possibly.'

'Of course you can. Calum won't care.'

With a sigh, Tiffany followed her. She'd wanted to make an impression on the heir to the House of Brodey, but this definitely wasn't what she'd intended.

Calum was waiting in a sitting-room looking out over the lawn where the tables were being cleared. Chris was with him. They stood up politely when the two girls came in. When they saw Tiffany in the over-sized robe, just her bare feet with pink-painted toes sticking out from under it, neither man could resist a grin.

She laughed and put out her arms as she twirled round. 'The latest creation from Paris,' she joked.

Stepping forward, Calum took her hand and said, 'Miss Dean, I'd like to apologise to you on behalf of my family. We're all extremely sorry that such a thing happened here.'

There was true regret in his tone, making Tiffany flush. Something made her glance towards Chris; he was watching them with a faintly mocking curl to his lip, and she immediately knew that she might have deceived Calum but not Chris. Trying to put things as right as possible, she said lightly, 'Oh, please, don't apologise. I probably over-reacted. After all, I had been sitting next to Mr Gallagher during lunch, and—well, in a way I suppose it's your fault really—you *do* serve excellent wine!'

Everyone laughed, even Chris's eyebrows rising in surprise, and the tension was immediately eased.

'And such a lot of it,' Francesca agreed.

'You're being extremely good about it,' Calum said, his lean features breaking into a warm smile. 'But you must let us make it up to you. Perhaps we could——'

But Francesca broke in, 'I know; you must join us for dinner tonight!'

Calum looked momentarily taken aback, but recovered quickly and smiled. 'Of course. Won't you join us for dinner, Miss Dean?'

It was what Tiffany had hoped and longed for, but she immediately protested, 'Oh, but I couldn't. I——'

'But you must,' Francesca broke in. 'We need someone to liven us up. Chris, come and persuade Tiffany to stay,' she commanded imperiously.

But Chris said, 'It will be dull with all the family there.'

'That's why she must come. Tiffany, please say you will.'

Pushing Chris's obvious reluctance out of her mind, Tiffany laughed and indicated the bathrobe. 'But how can I possibly?'

'Oh, that's easily solved. I'll ring a boutique in the town and tell them to bring up a selection of gowns for you to choose from. They should be here before too long,' Francesca said with all the confidence of a girl who only had to lift a phone to always get what she wanted. 'Now, you don't have any excuse, so please say that you'll stay.'

But Tiffany looked at Calum for reassurance, saying, 'I'm sure you really don't want an outsider at a family party.'

She got what she wanted. 'There will be others there beside ourselves. And you'll be very welcome, Miss Dean.'

Giving him one of her best smiles, she said, 'Well, if you're sure...'

'Quite sure. It will be a great pleasure.'

'Then I'd love to stay. But only——' she gave him a sparkling, playful look '—if you'll promise to call me Tiffany and not Miss Dean.' She imitated his deep voice, making Calum laugh.

'It's a bargain. I'll go and tell the caterer to change the table setting.'

'And I'll ring the boutique.' Calum went out and Francesca went over to the phone, but glanced at Tiffany and Chris and then said, 'The number is in my address book upstairs. Will you excuse me while I go and make the call?' And she hurried away.

Not wanting to be left alone with Chris, Tiffany said, 'I'll wait upstairs.' She went to follow Francesca out of the room, but got caught up in the skirts of the robe and had to hitch it up.

As she made for the door, Chris said, 'You're wasting your time, Tiffany.'

Pretending not to understand, she said over her shoulder, 'See you later.'

But Chris said sharply, 'You won't catch Calum.' She stopped, closed the door, which she had half opened, and turned to face him, leaning against it.

'I don't know what you mean.'

Chris laughed unpleasantly. 'You know *exactly* what I mean. Calum fell for your trick, but he's much too clever not to see through you eventually—even if no one tells him.'

He had jumped to the wrong conclusion, but it was impossible to tell him the truth; he would only have her thrown out that much more quickly if he knew she was trying to get a story on his cousin. 'Are you—are you threatening me?' she said unsteadily, the future looking a long, empty prospect again.

'No.' Chris straightened up from the arm of the settee on which he'd been sitting and came over to her. 'Just warning you that you'll be wasting your time.'

Tiffany thought of bluffing it out, but one look into Chris's eyes told her it would be no use. She didn't admit anything, but instead raised large, pleading eyes to his. 'Things have been tough for me lately. You wouldn't begin to understand . . .' Her fists clenched. 'I—I deserve a break.' She broke off, her voice unsteady.

Chris's mouth twisted sardonically, and she didn't think that she'd got through to him at all. But he amazed her by giving a shrug and saying, 'If you want to make a play for my cousin, then go ahead. Try your luck. But you'll be disappointed.'

'You mean you'll tell him anyway,' she said bitterly.

Slowly Chris shook his head. 'No, I won't tell him.'

Her eyes widened. 'But you said . . . Why won't you tell him?'

'I won't need to.' He put a hand under her chin. 'And maybe it will amuse me to watch you try.'

She stared at him, realising that he was playing with her. Her chin came up. 'All right—so watch.' Then she turned and walked out of the room with as much dignity as bare feet and a bathrobe could give her—which wasn't much.

CHAPTER TWO

FRANCESCA had told the boutique to send not only evening gowns but a choice of day clothes too. The assistant who had brought them was deferential to say the least. 'The Princess told us your size, *senhorita*, and that you were fair. I am sure you will find something here that you like.'

Tiffany was sure of it too; all of them looked good on her, and any one of the dresses, she was equally certain, would have put her in hock for the rest of her life. Not that any of the clothes had anything so vulgar as a price-tag attached. Wondering fleetingly if she was supposed to pay for the dresses, and deciding not to worry about it, Tiffany chose a chic blue shorts suit to wear for the rest of the day and a stunning black velvet cocktail dress to wear that evening. Luckily the boutique had also sent shoes and evening bags, so she was able to put a whole outfit together.

Francesca came in just as the assistant was packing up all the clothes, and applauded Tiffany's choice. 'Mmm. Nice. I wish I could wear those shorts suits, but my legs are so long I look ridiculous in them.' Patently untrue, of course, but it was a kind thing to say. 'Put the things on my account,' Francesca said offhandedly as the woman left.

'Oh, but really...' Tiffany made a half-hearted protest, comfortably sure that it would be overborne.

It was. Francesca lifted a hand to silence her. 'No, please. My pleasure. Let's go down, shall we?'

She was still wearing the flame outfit, and strode ahead down the corridor towards the stairs. After they'd gone about twenty yards, Tiffany called out, 'Hey! Do you always walk this fast?'

Pausing at the head of the staircase, Francesca laughed. 'Sorry. All my family are so tall that I suppose I'm not used to slowing down.'

'From what you said earlier, you don't seem to see much of them,' Tiffany remarked, coming up to her.

'Not as much as I'd like to. Especially Chris; he always seems to be somewhere I'm not, if you see what I mean.'

'Don't you live in Portugal?'

'No. I have an apartment in Rome, but at the moment I'm renting a house near Paris. And you?' she asked as they reached the bottom of the stairs and moved towards the sitting-room again. 'Do you live in Oporto?'

'Yes, I'm sharing a place with friends,' Tiffany returned, wondering what Francesca would think if she knew that 'sharing a place' really meant that someone she used to work with smuggled her in and out of an attic room shared with three other girls, and that Tiffany had only a sleeping-bag on the floor to call her own.

The room was empty, but the windows opened on to the garden and they could see Calum outside on the terrace, talking to the caterer again. The two girls went out to sit at an ornamental table and Calum brought the woman over to them.

'Francesca, do you have any further instructions for Mrs Beresford on the party at the *quinta*?'

'Yes. Would you excuse me a moment, Tiffany?'

The other girl moved away and Calum sat down beside Tiffany. He smiled. 'I see you found something to suit you.'

'Yes—much better than the bathrobe.'

'But you looked very pretty in it.'

She smiled at him under her lashes, having got the answer she wanted from him. 'Thank you.' Resting her chin on her hand, she looked at him attentively and said, 'Tell me; what is a *quinta*?'

She already knew, of course, but it was a good enough opening gambit.

'A *quinta* is the Portuguese word for farm or estate. It's where we grow the grape-vines for the port wine. I'm surprised you haven't come across it before.'

'But you see, my phrase-book only gives English to Portuguese; when it's the other way round I'm stuck.'

Calum laughed. 'I'll have to find you a two-way dictionary. That's if you're going to be here for very long?' He made it a question, which was a good sign.

'I don't have any immediate plans to leave. But you were telling me about your *quinta*; does it have a name?'

'The company owns several in the Alto Douro—that's the Upper Douro valley. Er—you do know that the river that runs through Oporto is the Rio Douro?'

'Oh, yes, I do know that,' she assured him with amusement in her eyes.

He nodded and gave a small smile. 'Our principal vine-growing estate is called the Quinta dos Colinas—the farm of the hills. That's where we're holding another bicentennial party, for all our workers and their families.'

'Do you actually make the wine at the *quinta*?'

'Yes, but by very modern methods. We no longer have workers treading the grapes to extract the juice.'

Tiffany's nose wrinkled a little. 'Why not?'

Reaching out, Calum tapped the end of her nose. 'For the very reason that you just did that! No one would buy the wine if they thought it had been trodden by the great feet of peasant workers. People are too particular today; everything must be done by hygienic methods.'

There was a slightly disparaging note in his voice which Tiffany picked up and used as a cue to say, 'I suppose so, but treading the grapes sounds much more romantic. Have you done it yourself?'

'Yes, but many years ago now.'

'Do you stand in a big tub to squash them? How high do they come up?'

'Not a tub, a big stone trough or tank. And on most people the grapes would come up to their knees, but on you I think it would be a little higher,' he remarked, looking at her legs.

'How unkind of you to remind me.'

'Do you dislike being short?'

'It's often a great disadvantage,' she admitted.

'I really can't see why you should think so.'

It was a nice reply, a compliment without going overboard. Tiffany began to realise that Calum must be more experienced with women than she'd thought. His reputation in Oporto wasn't that of a playboy—that title was reserved for Chris. From what she'd heard of him, Calum was the serious type, hard-working and rather reserved. He was also one of the most eligible bachelors in the town. Rich, very good-looking, well-bred—what girl could ask for more? And he was in his thirties—high time he went looking for a wife. But that wife would have to be fair, to carry on the Brodey tradition. Everyone knew that, so all the dark-haired girls, the brunettes and the redheads, sighed and left him alone, certain they would be wasting their time if they made a play for him. And there weren't too many blondes in Portugal, which was why Tiffany had thought him inexperienced. But that, of course, was stupid: even if the girl he eventually married had to be a blonde, that didn't stop him gaining experience with all the others.

He started to describe the first grape-treading he had been taken to, as a baby, still in his mother's arms. 'It's a tradition, you see. It's supposed to get wine-making into our blood.'

Behind them, Chris came out on to the terrace and overheard. Pulling out a chair, he turned it round to sit astride it, his arms along the back. 'But all it did was to give us a taste for wine from an early age. At least, it did in my case.'

Annoyed that he'd interrupted her tête-à-tête with Calum, Tiffany hid it behind a smile. 'I'm not surprised. But obviously it didn't work with your father.'

Chris raised an eyebrow. 'Who told you that?'

'Someone at your party said he was an artist, that he wasn't part of the family firm,' she said quickly, inwardly cursing herself for making such a stupid slip.

Calum nodded. 'That's so, but he still appreciates a good wine.'

Chris gave her an amused look. 'Who was it told you he was an artist?' he asked, guessing her thoughts, wanting to needle her.

But Tiffany was a match for him. 'Wasn't it you?' she said sweetly. A glint came into his eyes, but she turned quickly back to Calum. 'Are you interested in art, Calum? I'm afraid I know very little about Portuguese painters but I went to an exhibition recently at the museum. Did you go to it?'

'Yes. As a matter of fact our company was one of the organisers. A group has been formed to try to sponsor and encourage contemporary painters. Not that I agree with everything they do.'

'You don't like modern art?'

They got into a discussion on the subject, and she was on safe ground here because she really had been to the exhibition—when she'd read that Calum was one of the sponsors—and had also done a lot of reading since. She didn't overstate it, but could see that Calum was impressed by her knowledge. It was hard, though, to keep up her end of the conversation when out of the corner of her eye she could see Chris watching her, a sardonic curl of amusement to his lip, knowing exactly what the score was.

It was almost a relief when Francesca came back to join them and the conversation became general. She sat in between Calum and Chris, and they began to swap family stories and information, talking about people Tiffany had never heard of. Tiffany got to her feet. 'What time is dinner?'

'Oh, dear, don't let us drive you away, Tiffany. I'm sorry; it's just that we haven't seen each other for so long,' Francesca said, putting up a hand to stop her. 'We didn't mean to bore you. Chris, why don't you take Tiffany for a walk round the garden while I catch up on Calum's news? I'll get round to you later.'

'Oh, no, please. I'd just as soon——'

'But I insist,' Chris broke in. 'Francesca can tell me all her secrets later.'

'What makes you think I have any secrets?'

Chris bent to kiss her cheek. 'You always have—and until some man comes along who can tame you you always will.'

'Hark at the man! A psychologist now,' Francesca scoffed. 'I'll have you know I've decided to marry Michel.'

'Congratulations. I'll give it six months.'

'Six months!' Francesca exclaimed indignantly.

Chris gave her a contemplative look. 'No, perhaps you're right. *Three* months should have you bored to tears and walking out on him.'

Picking up a cushion, his cousin threw it at him, then pointedly turned her back. Chris chuckled and walked away, but Tiffany noticed that Francesca turned her head to look after him, a strange, desolate kind of look in her eyes.

Tiffany didn't want to be alone with Chris, was afraid that he would taunt her again, and had already decided that as soon as they were out of sight of the others she would make an excuse and leave him. But when they reached the far end of the lawn he said, 'I don't think you've seen the rest of the garden, have you? Let's go this way.'

'Thanks, but I'd really like to have a bath and change before dinner.'

Tiffany went to turn away but he reached out and put a firm hand under her elbow. 'There's plenty of time yet. Come and see the fruit garden.'

His grip was firm and Tiffany knew he wasn't about to let her go. She gave him an angry glare but had to go with him.

At the end of the ornamental garden there was what looked to be a very high, dense hedge sloping down the hill on which the house stood, but she was amazed to find that it was actually two hedges with a path that descended by flights of stairs between them. The hedges met overhead, giving a cool, shady walk, with occasional shafts of sunlight where there were openings into the garden. Stone seats were set into arbours and there were marble statues of wood-nymphs on plinths, the white stone standing out against the deep green of the hedges.

Tiffany gave an involuntary exclamation of surprise and delight. 'These gardens are magnificent! It must have taken years for these hedges to grow.'

'About a generation, I think,' Chris answered. 'My great-grandfather planted them for his wife. She was a Scot and found the climate of Portugal far too hot in the summer. Our ancestor, the original Calum Lennox Brodey who founded the House of Brodey, came from Scotland; that's why the names Calum and Lennox are always passed down the generations.'

Tiffany was silent for a moment, then said on a wry, wistful note, 'You and your cousins; you're really into ancestors and family traditions, aren't you?'

'You have something against that?' Chris turned his head to look at her, his eyes fixed on her face.

She gave a small shrug. 'Not really. It's just hard to understand when—when you've never experienced it before.'

'You have no family of your own?'

They reached the end of the green tunnel and emerged on to another terrace that looked out over the rest of the hill. In every direction the slopes were covered in fruit trees and bushes in neat rows, facing south, facing the sun, which was turning red now, beginning to set.

'Is all this your ground?' Tiffany asked, ignoring his question.

'It belongs to the house, yes. We've started diversifying by growing fruit for jam-making and preserves, that kind of thing.' Walking over to a nearby tree, Chris reached up to pick a bunch of cherries and brought them over to her. 'Here, try some.'

The cherries were deep red and fat. Tiffany put one into her mouth and bit through the skin. Juice, hot and sweet, spurted into her mouth, tasting like nectar. Closing her eyes, she gave herself up to the sensual pleasure of the taste on her tongue. She couldn't remember ever having had fruit straight from a tree before; it had always come cold and tasteless from a supermarket, when it could be afforded at all.

'Mmm, delicious.' She opened her eyes, took the stone from her mouth, and found Chris watching her with a look of sexual awareness in his eyes. It was a look that she had seen many times before and knew how to use, or not use, as she chose. And she certainly didn't have any use for it now, she thought with annoyance.

Flicking the stone away, she turned to go back, but Chris said, 'Wait,' and caught her wrist. 'You have juice on your mouth.' Tiffany lifted a finger to wipe it off, but he said softly, 'No, let me.' His eyes darkened and he bent to lick the juice away with his tongue.

Immediately Tiffany shoved him away. 'Keep away from me. And don't get any ideas,' she warned, blue eyes sparking angrily.

'But you looked so sexy.'

'How I look is no concern of yours.'

'Ah, saving yourself for Calum, are you?' Chris stepped back and put his hands in his pockets. 'You're aiming high, Tiffany.'

She tossed her head. 'And what's wrong with that?'

He shrugged. 'Nothing, I suppose. But you're not the kind of girl that Calum goes for—even if you are a blonde. Is that what gave you the idea of making a play for him; did you hear about the family tradition?'

Tiffany didn't answer, knowing there was no point in telling him she'd never heard of the tradition until she'd started reading up on the family. But she felt a surge of guilt because, once having read about it, she *had* thought that being blonde herself might help her to get to know Calum.

She flashed him a furious look that Chris immediately took as an answer in itself. He laughed shortly. 'I thought so. Do you know how many blonde girls—natural and dyed—have thrown themselves at Calum's head? A dozen of them. You can bet your life after an article mentioning the tradition has appeared in the Press some blonde will—accidentally—bump into one or other of us. It's become a family joke.'

Tiffany bit her lip. So much for a brilliantly original idea, she thought wryly. But then she remembered that she and Calum had seemed to get on well when they were alone together. When they were allowed to be alone together. Her chin coming up, she said, 'What makes you so sure of the type of girl he likes? You may be surprised.'

'I doubt it. Calum always plays it straight, and he abhors deceit. When he finds that you tricked your way into the party today, and slapped that poor American's face for nothing...' he shrugged eloquently '...you'll be out of here so fast you'll be choked by your own dust.'

'Just what are you saying?' Tiffany demanded. 'What do you want?'

'Why should I want something?'

'Men always want something,' Tiffany said with the certainty of long experience. She gave Chris a look of dislike. 'You tried to kiss me earlier and you didn't like it when I said no. You're telling me all this to threaten me. So that I'll beg you to keep quiet.'

'You did before,' Chris reminded her.

She shook her head. 'No, I asked you to give me a chance. But now you're trying to blackmail me. And what would the price be, I wonder?' she said jeeringly. 'For me to go to bed with you? To give myself to you so that you can get your own back for me saying no before?'

His head came up and Chris's eyes fastened on her. His jaw tensed, in anticipation, she thought, and for a moment he was silent, then he said, 'And your answer?'

The loathing in her eyes deepened as she said curtly, 'The answer's no! It always will be no. Go ahead, tell your cousin. I'd rather leave and walk all the way back to Oporto than go to bed with you!' She stood, short and fragile but full of defiance, her eyes alight with fury and her cheeks flushed as she faced up to him.

Chris's eyes were still fixed on her but he had taken his hands from his pockets and clenched them at his sides. Conflicting emotions seemed to chase across his face and it was a moment before he said tersely, 'You must know some very strange men, Tiffany.'

'What do you mean?'

'I mean,' he said curtly, 'that I also happen to play things straight, just like Calum. I said I'd give you a chance with him and I meant it. I have no intention of telling him about your scheming.'

Her mouth fell open. 'You—you won't tell him?'

'No! And for your information I don't have to resort to blackmail to get a girl I want. And, surprising as it may seem to you, I'm also civilised enough to take no for an answer without feeling any resentment.'

He stopped, as annoyed as she had been a moment ago, and all Tiffany could find to say was a faltering, 'I'm sorry.'

Chris ran an angry hand through his hair. 'Just who have you mixed with to make you think the way you do?'

'I'm sorry,' she said again.

He looked at her for a moment, then said, 'Come on, let's walk along here.'

He turned to the right, to a paved walk where a long, high brick wall divided the garden, shoring up the earth of the upper level and providing a sun-soaked backing for espalier fruit trees and climbing roses, all mixed in together. On the other side of the path were stakes that held up vines that spread themselves across wires attached to the wall, the bunches of grapes, still green and unripe, hanging down, waiting for the sun. The last bees of the day buzzed around the flowers, and butterflies in breathtaking colours fluttered against the deep flame of the setting sun. A beautiful, dream-like time and place.

The walk seemed to go on forever, but after a couple of hundred yards they tacitly decided to stop to look at the sunset. 'Do you want to tell me about it?' Chris asked after a while.

'About why I'm broke, you mean?' He nodded, and Tiffany sighed. 'It isn't a nice story. You really wouldn't want to hear it.'

'Try me.'

She hesitated, still not trusting him, then gave him an expurgated version. 'I was offered a job out here, down in the Algarve, as a kind of organiser and hostess at a swanky golf centre where a lot of English-speaking people came over on corporate hospitality trips, that kind of thing. It was OK for a while but then the hospitality company got hit by the recession and went bust, so I was out of a job with a couple of months' salary owing to me.' She paused, wondering if it would click in his mind, whether he would realise that it was the Brodey Corporation which was responsible. But his face showed absolutely no reaction; it didn't mean a thing to him that so many people had lost their livelihoods. Something close to hatred filling her, Tiffany added tersely, 'Then I got a job selling time-shares on a commission basis but I became ill and had to give it up.'

'What was the matter with you?'

She gave a short laugh. 'I got glandular fever of all things. I'd saved enough money for my fare, but the airlines said I was contagious and wouldn't fly me home. I was too ill to make the journey overland. So all my money went on the rent for a room, and by the time I was well enough to work again the time-share company had also gone into receivership.'

'So how did you end up in Oporto?'

'A girl who worked at the time-share development, a Portuguese girl, got a job here and thought there might be an opening for me as a guide. So I used up the last of my money to come here, but it didn't work out. Most of the tour companies want home-grown guides. I've been able to get a little work but it only pays enough money to live on.'

'So you thought you'd find yourself a rich husband,' Chris said with irony.

It was natural he should think that, Tiffany supposed, and she had to admit that seeing Calum, seeing this magnificent house, it had also been natural for the possibility of marriage to cross her own mind, too. But how to explain that to Chris? He wouldn't understand; what man would? To a man it was degrading for a woman to go in search of someone with money and deliberately set out to marry him. There were all kinds of phrases to describe it: running after a man, getting your hooks into one, selling yourself, gold-digging. But when you were in a strange country, without a job, hungry and desperate, it seemed like a very good idea. Especially when there was only one other easy way to make money that was open to an attractive girl. But to Tiffany the latter just wasn't an option, even though she was as low as she'd ever been. It wasn't as if she would sell herself short; if she married a man she would give darn good value for money, and be as loving and attentive as she knew how. He would have no cause to complain.

'Marriage is an older profession than prostitution,' she pointed out shortly.

He gave her a sharp glance, then said, 'If I offered you the fare home, would you go?'

Tiffany laughed. 'What would be the point? I have no place in England to go to, any more than I have here. Getting a job would be just as hard, finding a place to live probably impossible.'

'Don't you have any family?' he asked for the second time.

'No.' Tiffany turned and began to stride back along the path and through the garden, not looking to see whether Chris followed her or not, not giving him the chance to ask her any more questions.

They walked back to the house and Chris glanced at his watch. 'I suppose we might as well get ready for dinner. We meet for drinks in the drawing-room from seven-thirty.' He stayed by her side as they climbed the wide marble staircase and stopped at a door only three down from her own. 'See you later.'

There was a Jacuzzi in the bathroom opening off the guest room. Tiffany spent a good hour in it, only coming out when her skin began to wrinkle. She washed her hair again and took her time putting on her make-up and slipping into the beautiful black velvet dress. When she was ready she stood in front of the full-length mirror and knew that she had seldom in her life looked as good as this. Excitement filled her, all mixed up with optimism and hope, emotions that she hadn't felt for a very long time. But they frightened her. Experience had taught her not to hope because then the disappointment wouldn't be so great. But it was in her nature to be optimistic, and she looked so good now that it was impossible to stifle it.

It was almost eight when she left her room. There was the sound of voices echoing up from the hall as some guests arrived. Tiffany walked to the top of the staircase and stood there a moment, watching as Calum and his grandfather greeted their guests. It was like watching a film: the richly dressed people, the voices and laughter, the beautiful setting; Tiffany could hardly believe that she was to play a part in it, be a part of it.

Then Chris and Francesca came into the hall, arm in arm, laughing. Francesca let go and ran to kiss an elderly guest on the cheek. Chris followed, but something made him glance up and he saw Tiffany. He stood still, just as Calum followed his glance. For a supremely wonderful moment both cousins seemed frozen, gazing up at her. But then Tiffany smiled and came lightly down the stairs towards them.

Chris stepped back and let his cousin greet her. Calum took her hand and held it. 'You look enchanting.' His eyes smiled, were warm.

'Yes, that dress suits you.' Francesca came over and put a familiar hand on Calum's shoulder. 'Grandfather wants to know who Tiffany is. What shall we tell him, Tiffany?'

Outwardly Francesca was as warm and friendly as ever, but Tiffany's feminine intuition was tuned as finely as a Stradivarius and she immediately sensed a hidden antipathy in the other girl. Easy to sense but not easy to explain. Is she jealous because I look good? Tiffany wondered. Is she so vain that she doesn't like it if someone outclasses or equals her in looks? Tiffany decided it must be that, although Francesca, in a stunning silver sheath-dress, was just as eye-catching as she'd been that afternoon. Tiffany could understand feminine jealousy and dismissed it from her mind; she was determined to enjoy herself for once and wasn't about to let Francesca's petty emotions spoil it.

Calum took her over to meet his grandfather, introducing her merely as a friend, and then took her into the drawing-room where he got her a drink. She met his other cousin, Lennox, with his wife Stella, who was wearing a rich red maternity gown that really looked good on her. 'I suppose I would have looked more respectable in a dark colour,' she confided to Tiffany, 'but those might give my baby a sombre feeling and I want him to be warm and happy.'

'You're mad,' her husband told her, but kissed her lightly, a look of intense love in his eyes.

Francesca came over to them. 'You must come and meet Chris's parents,' she said, drawing Tiffany away. Glancing back, she said, 'Doesn't Stella look terrific? It almost makes you want to get pregnant.' Then, her voice altering fractionally, she added, 'Isn't it strange that Lennox is the only one—so far—of the younger generation of Brodeys to have married a blonde? Perhaps Chris and Calum are bored with all the hype the tradition has been given and with blondes of every shade continually chasing after them. I think they ought to break with it. Don't you agree?'

'Oh, absolutely,' Tiffany returned at once, returning fire with fire. 'How dated to let oneself be ruled by a family habit, especially when it comes to falling in love. Tell me, are there any traditions governing whom the women of your family can marry?'

'Oh, no. We're quite free to pick and choose,' Francesca returned, looking down at her with an arrested expression.

'Oh, that's good. I quite thought you had to start at the top of the aristocratic tree and work your way down.'

A gleam came into the taller girl's eyes and she gave a tight-lipped smile, but there was a contemplative look in the glance she gave Tiffany. She said nothing more, though, just took her over to meet Chris's parents, saying, 'This is Tiffany Dean, a friend of Chris's,' and then abandoning her to the two artists.

Drawing on that very useful art exhibition, Tiffany got on well with them and was still standing talking to them when dinner was announced. People began to pair up to go in, and Tiffany stood for a moment, wondering what she was supposed to do, but then Chris walked up to her and offered his arm. He pulled a comic face and said, 'Shall we join the queue?'

But when they got into the dining-room Tiffany found that she wasn't next to Chris. A card bearing her name, standing in a little silver holder, was at the end of the long table, next to that of Michel, Francesca's count. There was no one on her other side; old Mr Brodey was sitting in the centre of the long table, with his daughter, who was acting as the hostess, sitting opposite him. Chris frowned, but had no choice but to abandon her and go to his place at the far end of the table, next to Francesca. Michel didn't look at all pleased. He hesitated, almost moved to speak to Francesca, but then changed his mind and came to sit down next to Tiffany. It didn't take much guessing to realise that Francesca had switched the name cards, to both men's annoyance. Tiffany couldn't understand why she was being so petty, until it occurred to her that Chris might have told Francesca that she'd gatecrashed the lunch party. Then she wasn't at all sorry not to be sitting next to Chris and, to annoy them both, she put herself out to charm and amuse the Count, speaking to him in French.

'You know France?' he asked.

'Oh, yes,' she answered. 'I lived there for some time.'
She didn't find it necessary to tell him that she had been
there to work, picking fruit on a farm.

Perhaps Michel, too, was annoyed with Francesca,
because he seemed very willing to talk and laugh, seldom
turning to talk to the woman on his other side, outwardly appearing to be well-pleased where he was.

The food, again, was some of the best Tiffany had
tasted in months, but the meal seemed to go on for a
long time, with several toasts, and a speech by old Mr
Brodey. When it was over at last, Michel pulled her chair
out for her and escorted Tiffany back into the drawing-
room. She had been afraid that the men might stay
behind to pass the port bottle round, but was relieved
to find that they weren't that old-fashioned.

Calum brought a cup of coffee over to her. 'I hope
you weren't too bored by all that,' he said with one of
his warm smiles.

'Not at all. Michel was a most entertaining dinner
companion.'

The Count smiled and gave a very Gallic bow. 'And
I must return the compliment. The time flew by.' Calum
didn't move on. Michel looked at them both, then went
to get himself a coffee.

'I'm sorry you were seated at the end of the table,'
Calum said, a slight frown in his eyes.

Tiffany shrugged. 'In the circumstances it was kind
of you to include me in your party at all.'

He stayed to chat with her and, having had a few
glasses of wine, Tiffany was at her wittiest, making him
laugh and keeping him by her side for quite a while. It
was only when someone came up to speak to him that
he moved reluctantly away.

Half an hour or so later the party began to break up,
Lennox and his wife being the first to leave. Many of

the guests were staying in the house, but the others were saying a leisurely goodbye before going to their cars. Tiffany hesitated, not knowing quite what to do, realising unhappily that she didn't have enough money for the taxi fare.

Francesca glanced at her, then walked over. 'Michel is going into Oporto, Tiffany. He can take you home. I'm sure you'll find something terribly amusing to talk about on the way.'

Michel was looking angry, his face set, as if they'd had a row, but he said courteously, 'Of course. It will be my pleasure.'

But Calum said, 'That's kind of you, Count, but Tiffany is our guest; we'll see that she gets home safely.'

'But you've been drinking; you can't possibly take her,' Francesca protested. 'Let Chris take her.'

'Chris has been drinking too,' Calum said calmly. 'But my chauffeur hasn't.' He smiled at Tiffany. 'Shall we go?'

Her heart swelled with pleasure and excitement, so much that it was hard to hide it, to play it cool. 'Well, if you're sure...'

'Of course.' He held the door open for her.

Tiffany glanced back and saw Chris and Francesca standing together in the hall. Francesca looked plainly annoyed, but there was a strangely strained look in Chris's eyes. Turning away, Tiffany followed Calum out to the car.

'I'm afraid your cousin doesn't like me very much,' she remarked as the big car glided away.

'Chris?' He sounded surprised.

'No, Francesca.'

Calum laughed rather ruefully. 'The poor girl isn't very happy at the moment. She's unsettled, still smarting from her divorce. And she seems to have lost her way.' He paused reflectively. 'Maybe what she needs is a friend.'

Tiffany hoped he wasn't considering her for the role: two girls of such different heights would look ridiculous going around together. And anyway, she rather thought that Chris had been right; what Francesca needed was a man to tame her.

'Where do you live?' Calum asked her.

She was ready for that one and named a respectable apartment block, not too far away from the boarding house in distance but light-years in rent and facilities.

'How do you come to be in Oporto?'

She gave a light laugh. 'I'm a victim of circumstance. I like to travel, so I took a job as a corporate hospitality arranger at a complex in the Algarve. But then I became ill so I came to stay with friends in Oporto.' Deliberately, she gave a very sketchy version of the truth, but it didn't sound too bad, put like that.

'And I believe you work in Oporto now?'

Tiffany nodded. 'Not that you can really call it work. I help out with entertaining English visitors to some of the commercial companies in the town.'

She had expected these questions; Calum was bound to ask them. The light was out in the car and there were no street-lights here so it was difficult to see what impression her answers had made. She could only hope that her looks and personality had made a greater one and that he was interested enough in her not to care too much about her background. But he didn't attempt to make a pass, didn't even take her hand or anything. Not just because the chauffeur was there, she guessed, but because he was too civilised by nature.

'Do you have any more celebrations tomorrow?' she asked him.

'Yes, in the evening we're going to broach a special pipe of port that was laid down fifty years ago.'

'A pipe?'

'Sorry, that's a measurement of wine. It's——' He broke off as the car telephone rang. 'Excuse me.' He picked up the phone, murmured, 'Yes?' and listened, then replaced it. 'That was Francesca. She said you left some clothes behind at the house.'

'Oh, of course. How stupid of me!' Tiffany exclaimed.

Calum smiled. 'She suggests you go back for them tomorrow afternoon at three o'clock.'

They came to the apartment block and the car pulled up. Calum helped her out and walked into the foyer with her. 'You'll be all right from here?'

'Of course. Thank you for bringing me home.'

'It was my pleasure. Goodnight.' He went to go, then turned back. 'Tomorrow afternoon—don't worry about getting to the house; I'll send a car for you. Goodnight, Tiffany.'

When he'd gone, Tiffany waited a few minutes, then walked round to the boarding house. There was a light on in the room she illicitly shared. She threw some pebbles up at the window and one of the girls opened it, leaned out and dropped the keys down to her. The lock and hinges of the entrance door were well-oiled, they'd seen to that; none of them squeaked when she let herself in and climbed silently up the stairs, thanking her stars that the landlord usually drank himself to sleep every night. She undressed, carefully hanging up the velvet dress, then slipped into her sleeping-bag, thinking that her luck had changed at last.

On the pavement outside, the watcher saw the light go out, then walked to the waiting car and drove back to the *palácio*.

CHAPTER THREE

THE gardens of the *palácio* seemed strangely empty without the tables and their sun umbrellas when Tiffany arrived there the next afternoon. She was still on a high, still daring to hope that her luck had changed. The driver had picked her up at three exactly from the apartment building where she had been on the look-out for him. Not knowing whether Calum would be there or not, not really knowing if she would see any of the family, Tiffany had nevertheless dressed carefully in an outfit left over from her days as hostess at the golf club, smart but not flashy, chosen with unerring taste for what suited her.

A maid opened the door of the house as soon as the car drew up at the entrance. The chauffeur hastened to open the car door, and Tiffany walked inside thinking that she could soon get used to all this attention. The maid led her to a room at the back of the house. There were sofas and chairs, but it was more a working-room, this, with a large desk in the centre and bookshelves lining the walls. All three cousins were there. Calum and Chris were seated at the desk, going through some papers, Francesca was sitting with her feet up on a sofa, reading a magazine. She looked up when Tiffany was shown in, but stayed where she was. Calum rose and came forward with a smile of greeting, but Chris's eyes widened, as if he hadn't known she was expected.

'Nice to see you again, Tiffany. Would you like a drink?' Calum asked her.

55

'Thank you. A coffee would be nice.' Calum spoke to the maid in Portuguese, and Tiffany said, 'Hi, Francesca. Chris.'

Chris had got to his feet, but now he half sat on the edge of the desk, a slight frown between his brows as he said, 'Hello, Tiffany. A surprise visit?'

'No, I asked her to call,' Francesca said, getting languidly to her feet. 'She left her clothes behind last night.' She turned to Tiffany. 'You'll be glad to hear that the wine came out of your suit; it hasn't left a mark.'

'Oh, good,' Tiffany said with relief. 'Will you thank your maid for doing it for me?' She reached for her bag. 'Perhaps I can give her something...'

But Francesca waved the idea away. 'Of course not. It was our pleasure.' She smiled at Tiffany, but there was no longer any warmth in it, and Tiffany braced herself to meet some kind of challenge. But Francesca began to chat about the other festivities they'd arranged for that week, which were to peak with a ball to be held at the best hotel in Oporto. 'We would have liked to hold the ball here, but the hotel is the only place that's big enough to hold all our guests.'

She chattered on rather aimlessly, and Tiffany, who had at first felt relieved, began to feel rather uneasy. Francesca didn't seem to have all her attention on what she was saying; it was almost as if she was waiting for something.

Calum was gathering up the papers on his desk, putting them into a folder. 'We'll finish going through these figures tomorrow,' he said to Chris. The maid arrived with the coffee-tray and set it down on a table by the window. 'I seem to remember you take yours black, don't you, Tiffany?'

'Yes.' She smiled at him, inordinately pleased that he had remembered, feeling a frisson of excitement as she looked at his tall, handsome figure as he bent to pour the coffee.

'Of course, this is really Francesca's job, but she refuses to——'

He broke off as the door opened again. The maid said, 'Senhor Gallagher,' and for the second time Sam walked in when he wasn't wanted.

Calum straightened with the coffee-pot still in his hand, surprise and then a frown coming into his face. Chris, too, was taken by surprise, but Sam's arrival was obviously what Francesca had been waiting for, because she went to him and said, 'Mr Gallagher. Thank you so much for coming. We wanted to——'

But Sam had seen Tiffany, and said, 'What is this?'

'Yes.' Calum put down the pot and looked at his cousin, his chin jutting forward grimly. 'Just what *is* Mr Gallagher doing here, Francesca?'

But the Princess waited until the maid had gone before she said, 'I asked him to come here because our family has done him an injustice and we owe him an apology.'

Sam began to say, 'That wasn't why I came here. I——'

But Calum held up an imperious hand. 'And just why does he deserve an apology from us? Surely it should be the other way round? It was Mr Gallagher who abused our hospitality by his boorish behaviour to one of our guests.'

Tiffany had been standing rooted to the spot, knowing it was all about to blow up in her face again, but now she made a faint sound of protest at the way he'd spoken of Sam. 'No, please.'

Ignoring her, Calum said, 'Well, Francesca?'

'That's just it,' his cousin replied. 'Tiffany wasn't our guest—not officially. She wasn't invited, and I very much doubt if anyone passed an invitation on to her as she said. Last night I looked in her bag and there was no invitation in it.'

'You looked through my bag?' Tiffany gasped, her face going pale.

'To find out your address so I could send your clothes on to you,' Francesca answered with a defiant lift of her chin. 'Only there was no address there.'

She went to go on but Chris intervened. 'Leave this, Francesca,' he said sharply. 'Let it go.'

'But that wouldn't be fair,' his cousin protested. 'And nor was the way we treated Mr Gallagher. It's Tiffany who's a liar and a cheat. When I began to suspect that she'd gatecrashed the party, I tracked Sam down and he admitted that she'd lied about the incident, that he hadn't made a pass at her. But he accepted the situation because he didn't want to get Tiffany into trouble——'

'That wasn't how I remember it went,' Sam cut across her. 'As far as I'm concerned that incident was closed yesterday. And I don't like the way you're doing this, Princess,' he said angrily.

He turned as if to go, but Calum, his voice very cold, said, 'Just one moment. I think we need to get to the bottom of this.' He paused, his face tight, then slowly turned to Tiffany. 'I have to ask you——'

She interrupted him, her face pale and set. 'No, you don't have to ask me any questions. I admit it. It's all true. I did gatecrash your party. And I did lie about Sam. I'm sorry about that.' Her head came up. 'But I'm not sorry about anything else. I meant to gatecrash your party and I did it.' Looking at Calum, she gave a small smile. 'I wanted to meet you, you see.'

'Because you read about the stupid tradition, I suppose,' Calum said angrily. 'You're just another scheming chit out for what you can get.'

Two spots of colour appeared on Tiffany's white cheeks. 'Yes, I suppose I am—in your eyes. But your eyes are very biased, very blasé. All I was looking for was a chance. How else is a girl like me supposed to meet a man like you?'

'Hopefully you never will, if this is how your type behaves,' Calum bit out scathingly.

He went to turn away, open disdain in his eyes, but Tiffany caught his sleeve and said furiously, 'Now just you wait a minute! What the hell do you know about "my type"? You sit here in your icing-sugar palace with two hundred years of ancestors stuck on the walls, and you think you have the right to judge me and others like me. What do you know about grief and pain and hunger? When did you ever have to go without anything you ever wanted: another car, another sail-boat, *anything* in your life?' Her eyes swept round the three cousins, her eyes flashing fire. 'You're all nothing but rich, spoilt parasites. Especially you!' Tiffany's finger came up to point accusingly at Francesca. 'I hope the Count has more sense than to marry you, because he's too darn good for you.' Her head lifting proudly, spitting fury, she glared at Calum and added, 'Just as I'm too good for you!'

Her voice came to a stop and for a moment there was a shocked silence in the room, then everyone but Chris moved or spoke at once. He just stood there, looking stunned. Francesca began to say indignantly, 'Well, really! Of all the nerve. It was you who——'

But Calum pulled himself together and swung to face Sam. 'Mr Gallagher, I have to make you the most profound apology. It seems that I have been tricked and duped, allowed myself to be taken in by a pretty face. I should have known better. I'm grateful to Francesca for finding out the truth and giving me this opportunity to put things right.'

'I didn't ask for any apology and I don't want it,' Sam returned shortly. 'Tiffany, wait for me outside. I'll take you back to town.' He gave Francesca a menacing look. 'But first I want to have a word with the Princess!' And, taking hold of Francesca by the wrist, he strode through the open French windows, pulling her behind him.

Ignoring Sam's offer, Calum said with freezing politeness, 'I'll have my chauffeur drive you home.'

It would have done Tiffany's pride a great deal of good to have refused, but it wouldn't do her dignity any good to try to walk all the way back to Oporto, and she certainly didn't intend to stand around waiting for Sam. So, her voice equally cold, she said, 'Thank you. Where are my things?'

'I believe Francesca has them ready for you in the room you used yesterday. I'll send a maid to get them.'

'Don't bother; I'll get them myself.' And without giving him the opportunity to protest Tiffany ran up the stairs and along the corridor.

Her clothes had been carefully packed between layers of tissue-paper into a large dress-box. Not only the grey silk suit and her handbag, but also the outfit she'd worn yesterday afternoon, along with the accessories that went with it. Tiffany pulled out the latter and threw them on the bed; no way was she going to be beholden to Francesca. She fumbled to do the dress-box up again, but found that her hands were shaking and she couldn't see because tears of mingled anger and despair threatened to engulf her. 'Oh, hell!' She stood still for a minute, fighting them back, determined not to let them see her cry.

The door opened behind her and she thought it was Calum, come to order her out of the house. But it was Chris.

Shutting the door, he walked towards her, saying quickly, 'Tiffany I'm sorry it happened this way. I——'

'Don't lie!' She swung round on him furiously. 'Do you think I don't see through you? Francesca didn't work all that out for herself; she hasn't got the brains. You told her! You told her because I turned you down. And you planned it to happen this way, to hurt and humiliate me just as much as you could.'

'No! Listen to me; I——'

'Don't lie!' she yelled at him again. 'You were the one who walked Sam out of the house yesterday, talked to him. That's why you were so sure about me. Calum called *me* a liar and cheat, but *you* lied to me and *you* cheated me! You said you'd give me a chance with him, but you and your rotten cousin were planning this all along. Did it amuse you? Did the two of you laugh about it together? Did your cruel, perverted minds get a kick out of——?'

'Tiffany, I did not plan this.' Striding up to her, Chris took her by the shoulders and looked down at her earnestly. 'I swear it.'

She laughed in his face, derision and disbelief mingled in the harsh sound. A flash of anger came into Chris's eyes and his hands tightened as he gave her an impatient shake. 'Will you simmer down and listen for a minute?'

'Why the hell should I?'

'Because I didn't have any hand in this. I didn't have to. It was inevitable that you were going to be found out. It was just a question of when and who by. I already warned you that Calum was no fool.'

'So you just sat there and let them get on with it. Thanks a lot!' She tried to push him away but he wouldn't let go.

'Yes. Sure I did,' Chris said forcefully. 'It had to happen so I let it. You knew the score. You knew what would happen when you were found out.' He gave a short laugh. 'Did you really think that Calum would be so bowled over by you in so short a time that he would overlook being lied to?'

Tiffany's face tightened in both anger and guilt. 'Stranger things have happened,' she said shortly.

Chris looked down at her, an odd, ironic look in his eyes. 'Maybe they have at that.'

Managing to push him away, she picked up the box and made for the door.

'Tiffany!' His voice halted her for a second. 'You haven't lost out completely.' She turned and looked at him and he gave a wry grin. 'You may have blown it with Calum—but there's still me.'

'*You*!'

The way she said it, her voice heavy with disdain, made his mouth tighten, but Chris merely gave her back her own words. 'Stranger things have happened.'

She stared at him, then said, 'Is this a proposal of marriage?'

'Of course not.'

'That's what I thought.' Her voice was heavy with contempt, letting him know just what she thought of him.

'What have you got to lose?'

'A great deal—not that I expect you to understand that.'

The grim look around his mouth deepened, but Chris said, 'Think about it.'

Giving him a look of loathing, Tiffany said, 'I don't have to—I'd rather die.' Then she turned and strode away.

Calum's car was waiting for her outside but there was no sign of Sam, so Tiffany got into it. She didn't look back at the house as she was driven away; she wished now that she'd never seen it, never agreed to accept the assignment, never met Calum. Not that way, at least. But if only she could have met him in different circumstances... Because he had been attracted to her. He had. He had! For a moment she let herself imagine what it would have been like if Calum had fallen in love with her and married her. What it would have been like to be mistress of that house, to be able to stroll in that lovely garden whenever she wanted to, to rest on the stone seats in the hedge walk, to reach up and pick cherries from her own trees. But that was just a stupid, impossible dream, as stupid and impossible as her impulsive attempt to attain it.

The driver dropped her off at the apartment block and she let him get out of sight before she walked away. It was too early yet to go back to the boarding house; the landlord would still be around, awake from his lunchtime siesta that went on half the afternoon, but not ready to stroll down to his favourite bar to eat his supper and drink for the rest of the evening.

Tiffany took the suit back to the hire shop, got her precious deposit back and began to walk aimlessly through the town. It was a thing she often did when she had to keep out of the landlord's way, and usually she loved it, fascinated by seeing old buildings down narrow alleyways, iron balconies hung with washing and with pretty flower-boxes, and tiny cafés like warm, inviting caves. But today nothing could lift her spirits, not even the huge central market with its hundreds of colourful stalls. A lot of the stalls were empty now, the holders having sold their produce and gone home after the morning rush, but there were still enough of them and

ample customers to make it a noisy, echoing place as
people bartered for fruit and clothes, for exotic-looking
vegetables and cured meat and fish.

To cheer herself up, Tiffany rashly blew some of her
money on a bunch of pink carnations, and the stall-
holder gave her a rose as well, making her smile at him.
Back in the town again, she passed pastry shops, the
windows piled with tarts and mouth-watering cakes,
making her feel hungry. But she had eaten really well
yesterday, courtesy of the Brodeys, she thought grimly,
so contented herself with buying a couple of rolls and
some ham.

She ate them slowly, washed down by a canned drink,
sitting on a seat that overlooked the river. On the opposite bank, at Vila Nova de Gaia, she could see all the
port wine cellars owned by the different wine companies,
many of them with their names emblazoned on the roofs
or on huge signs, 'BRODEY'S' prominent among them.
It was there that the tourists went to taste the port vin-
tages and to buy wine to take home. It was beyond these
buildings, further into the hills, that the Brodeys' *palácio*
lay. There was, it seemed, no getting away from them.
Even when she looked down at the river she could see
the row of moored *barcos rabelos*, the boats, shaped
rather like Viking ships, that used to bring the great
barrels of wine down the river from the *quintas* to the
wine cellars, there to be matured and bottled. Each of
the port wine houses owned one of the barges, and every
year they had a race down from the harbour bar to the
main quay in the town. It must be quite a sight, she
thought, and wondered whether she would ever see it,
what her future held, whether she would ever have anything that could be called a future instead of a day-to-
day existence.

Now that she'd blown the magazine assignment, she had absolutely no prospect of being able to earn any money. There just weren't any jobs available. There was always the offer that Chris had made her, of course, but it only crossed her mind for the briefest moment. Tiffany still strongly suspected that he had had a hand in betraying her to Calum, even though he'd sworn that he hadn't. But you couldn't trust a man's word; Tiffany had learnt that long ago. Although she had to admit that she had been tempted to with Chris. He had seemed so genuine. But he had been far cleverer than she, exposing her, and then making that offer when she was down. But she wasn't that down, not yet!

Resolutely turning her back on the river, Tiffany determined not to be so gloomy. After all, what had she lost? Just the hire of the suit, that was all. And she'd gained two very good meals, which was definitely a plus. And maybe she *could* even get a magazine article out of it, about the beauty and décor of the *palácio*, or something. Finding a phone booth, she rang the editor in Lisbon and tried to sell him the idea, but he was interested only in the Brodeys themselves and turned down the idea, so she was again without hope. Waiting until she was sure the landlord would have gone out, Tiffany got to her feet and walked dejectedly to the boarding house.

It was the middle of the night when the door was flung open and the light switched on. The girls sat up, startled into wakefulness, blinking owlishly. The landlord stood in the doorway. He gestured to where Tiffany lay on the floor in her sleeping-bag and started shouting and waving his arms around.

Tiffany had been learning Portuguese but she wasn't fluent enough to follow his storm of anger. Not that she needed to; it was perfectly obvious that he had suspected she was there and had decided to find out. He seemed to be yelling at her to get up and clear out, right now! The three Portuguese girls added their voices, arguing and cajoling, until a heated argument developed. Then suddenly the girls fell silent, glaring at the landlord mutinously. Knowing he had gained the upper hand, that they were cowed beneath his threats, the man shouted a couple of last, triumphant sentences, then walked out of the door, slamming it behind him.

Angry voices sounded from other residents who had been disturbed, and they heard the landlord talking loudly to them before he went clumping back down the stairs. He must have absolutely crept up them, despite his huge bulk, to have surprised them so completely.

Tiffany began to get up, saying dully, 'I'll get my things together.'

'No, no,' Isabel said quickly. 'We 'ave persuaded 'im to let you stay until tomorrow morning. It would be cruel to make you go tonight.'

'We tried to make him let you stay all the time,' one of the other girls added. 'But he said unless you go we all go.'

'I guessed that,' Tiffany said with a sigh. 'It was kind of you. But you mustn't risk losing this place.'

'We will think of somewhere you can stay,' the girls assured her.

Tiffany didn't sleep much for the rest of the night, and when morning came she grimly packed her one big suitcase and went downstairs with the girls. Usually the landlord was never up this early, but he was waiting to make sure that she left. He shouted at her again, but Tiffany just shrugged. '*Não compreenda.*'

She turned to Isabel. 'Tell him I'm very sorry but I had nowhere else to go, will you? And—and ask him how he found out I was here.'

Her apology made the landlord only a little less surly, and he was reluctant to answer her question, but eventually said that 'someone had told him', but he wouldn't say who, and got angry again when Tiffany got Isabel to press him.

Taking it in turns to carry her heavy case, they walked to the post office and Tiffany waited while they all rang their contacts, eventually coming triumphantly out of the booth with the news that they had found her a room in a house quite near to the main quay. It was in the very oldest part of the town, a place of tall houses crowded together in narrow streets, layer upon layer of floors, some decorated with the traditional blue tiles on the walls, some painted, most of them with peeling walls and sun-baked woodwork. A place that looked quaint and picturesque from the outside, but was not at all pleasant to live in. As Tiffany soon found.

The 'room' was on the top floor and little larger than a cupboard. She had to share the kitchen and extremely antiquated bathroom facilities with everyone else in the house. As there seemed to be dozens of little rooms like hers, some of them lived in by whole families, she never got more than five minutes in the bathroom before someone was banging on the door, demanding that she hurry. Some woman or other was always cooking throughout the day, so that the smells permeated the walls, competing with the stink from the communal lavatory. The sheets were visibly unclean, and Tiffany had to wash them in cold water and dry them out of the window before she would even consider lying on them. The whole house made her cringe with distaste, but there was nothing she could do about it; she had been lucky to find the room, and it was all she could afford.

Despite her lack of money, the first thing Tiffany did was to buy paper and string so that she could parcel up

the black velvet dress and send it back to Francesca.
That done, she smartened herself up as best she could
and set out to visit every hotel in Oporto, asking for
work. Three days later she was still looking. She had
been to every hotel within walking and tram distance
and had spent hours in a phone booth calling those
outside the district. Her poor Portuguese hadn't helped,
it had taken nearly every escudo she possessed, and all
she had gained was the promise of an interview in a few
months' time at a monastery an hour's train journey
away down the Douro valley which was in the process
of being turned into a super-luxury hotel.

When she went back to her room that night, Tiffany
knew that she had reached rock-bottom. She thought of
applying to the British Consulate, but she had tried them
when she was ill with glandular fever, and they had insisted on her sending a doctor's certificate, wanted to
know how much money she had, what she was doing in
Portugal, whether she was living with anyone, and on
and on. It had made Tiffany feel like a beggar, and the
process had been so slow that in the end she had recovered before she got any help from them.

The area was noisy with traffic and the sound of the
floating discos across the river. Even when they were
over she was unable to sleep because all the babies in
the house seemed to take it in turns to cry throughout
the night. Wearily, Tiffany got up in the mornings feeling
itchy and unclean, her only consolation being that when
she'd been to the first hotel to try for a job she'd been
able to go in the ladies' room and wash all the bits of
herself she could reach.

She tried to think of what she could do, whether there
was anywhere else she could try for work. There was
certainly no one to whom she could go for help; she had
seen Isabel and the girls and they had bought her a meal,

despite her protests, but she definitely couldn't sponge on them again. They had done and risked enough for her already. The thought of Sam Gallagher crossed her mind, but she had no right to ask him for help. And anyway, he might have left Portugal by now.

Which left only one alternative.

Tiffany bit her lip hard, fighting despondency. She gave it another day, walking all the way across the long Dom Luis bridge across the river to Vila Nova de Gaia to try again at the wine cellars for a job, a route she had last travelled in Calum's limo. She had already tried them all on the phone—all except Brodey's, of course—so it was a last desperate try. But there were enough Portuguese people out of work to fill every job, enough who could speak English to take the jobs as guides and wine-sellers. She came away without having had any luck, walked back into town, and tried every shop and business place she passed until the shops and offices closed.

Sitting down in the square by the river, Tiffany went through her handbag, stuffed with everything that was of any value to her because the key of her room was lost, took the last of her money from her purse and counted it. It didn't take long. She was paying for the room by the day and there was just enough for one more night—or for a phone call. For a long time she just stared down at the money in her hand, wondering what to do, whether a miracle might happen. But the world seemed to be short on miracles, as far as she was concerned anyway.

A man, a middle-aged Portuguese, came up and spoke to her. Tiffany didn't understand what he said, but she only had to glance at the lascivious smile on his fat face to know what he wanted. It seemed that there were two choices after all. Getting to her feet, she shook her head at the man and strode away to the nearest telephone booth.

It took a while for the phone to be answered. Working out what day it was, Tiffany remembered that there was to be a dinner party for fellow wine-growers at the Brodey *palácio* that evening. Presumably it would already have started.

This was confirmed when the butler answered the phone and she asked for Chris.

'I am sorry. Senhor Brodey is not available.'

'This is a very important call. He will be extremely angry if you don't tell him,' Tiffany said curtly.

The butler protested but she insisted and he eventually went away to find Chris.

It was several minutes before he came to the phone and she had to feed more money into the box, uneasily wondering whether she would have enough.

'Christopher Brodey here.'

At the sound of his voice Tiffany almost put the phone down, almost lost her nerve. But then she forced herself to say, the words coming out abruptly, 'I thought about it.'

There was dead silence on the line. A silence that went on for so long that Tiffany thought he must have changed his mind. But then he said shortly, 'And?'

'There are conditions I would need to discuss.'

'Where and when?'

'The little square in Ribeira, the one with the modern cube sculpture. Do you know it?'

'Yes. When?'

'Now.'

'Now is hardly convenient.'

'Make it convenient,' Tiffany said shortly, and put down the phone.

Walking back to the square, she sat down to wait at one of the café tables and ordered a coffee with the last of her money. She felt that she had condemned her future to fate. If Chris wanted her badly enough then he would come, but if he didn't... She shrugged mentally, suddenly too weary and desolate to care any more.

It took about twenty minutes to drive into Oporto from the *palácio*, so Tiffany had expected to wait at least half an hour for Chris to come, if he came. But it was nearly an hour later, and she had just about given him up, when he walked into the square and paused to look round for her. He was wearing an evening suit and dress tie, looking completely out of place—not that he seemed to care. Coming across to her table, he pulled up a chair and sat opposite her. His eyes were on her face, but she didn't care that he could see the dark shadows of tiredness around her eyes, the pinched look of her cheeks from hunger. It took an effort to raise her own eyes to meet his, because she wasn't sure what to expect. Triumph perhaps, pleasure in his easy victory at least.

But Chris betrayed no emotion, either in his face or eyes. His features seemed to be as enigmatic as those of a costume mask as he said, 'Hello, Tiffany.' She nodded but didn't speak, so after a moment he said, 'What are the conditions?'

'I want a whole new wardrobe.'

His mouth quirked a little. 'Of course.'

'Decent clothes,' she warned him.

'Naturally.'

'And I want a thousand pounds when—when you grow tired of me.'

Something flickered in his eyes, but he said, 'All right.'

That had been easy, very easy, but Tiffany knew that he wouldn't be so amenable to her next condition. Lifting her chin defiantly, she said, 'And I want to go to the celebration ball tomorrow to mark your family's bicentennial.'

Chris's eyes came swiftly to her face. 'Why?'

She hesitated, not sure of her own reasons, and Chris said curtly, 'If you still think you can make a play for Calum——'

'No!' Her frowning denial was too emphatic to be false. 'I don't really know why. For my own self-esteem...' She looked at him and gave an ironical laugh. 'No, not for that. I just know I *need* to go there.'

'To make a scene? To spoil the party for us?'

'No. I promise I won't do that. You have no reason to be afraid.'

Chris looked at her keenly and she returned his gaze steadily until he nodded. 'All right. I'll take you. Is there anything else?'

'No, that's it.'

Still watching her, he said on an odd note, 'And just what do I get in return for all this?'

She looked at him, swallowed. 'I'll—I'll be anything you want me to be.' Her eyes met his, saw the concupiscence that her answer had awakened and quickly looked away.

He stood up. 'Where are you staying? Let's go and collect your things.'

Tiffany thought of the suitcase of old clothes, and shoes worn down by trailing round the town for the last few days. 'I don't need them; you've promised to buy me new ones.'

His eyebrows rose. 'But what about your personal possessions?'

She patted her handbag. 'Everything I value is in here.'

Disbelief in his voice, Chris said, 'But no woman could possibly——'

'Why do you think I phoned you?' Tiffany interrupted shortly.

He stared at her and his face became even more shuttered as he said, 'I was the last resort, was I?'

'Yes,' she answered, not caring, perhaps even wanting to goad him into changing his mind.

For a moment she thought that he was going to call the whole thing off, and she held her breath, wondering which way fate would jump. But suddenly he grinned. 'Well, I suppose it's as well to know where one stands from the start. Let's go. My car is down in the car park by the river.'

She expected him to have a fast sports car, but he led her to an ordinary saloon, and she leaned back in the seat as he drove away.

'Don't you want to know where we're going?' Chris asked after a few minutes.

Now that it was all settled, the nervous energy that had sustained her had drained away, and Tiffany was just too tired to care. 'To a hotel, I suppose,' she answered drearily.

'No. I've arranged somewhere else for you. An apartment. That's why I took so long to get here. I had to collect the key.'

Tiffany was silent, thinking that he must have been very sure of her. And of himself. He hadn't even known what conditions she would make when he'd come to meet her tonight. So he must want her very badly if he had been prepared to agree to anything she asked.

'I'm afraid I'll have to drop you off there. I have to get back to the house,' Chris was saying.

She turned her head away, not wanting to look at him, expecting him to say that he would come back after the party. To claim her. To sample what he had bought.

They didn't speak again until they reached the apartment block. It was a modern one in the most luxurious part of the town, near the beaches. Chris came up with her in the lift and unlocked the door, switched on the lights, then waited while she looked into the rooms.

It was a beautiful place, like a photo-spread in a glossy monthly, all neutral shades of beige, with thick pile carpet and deep, comfortable chairs. There was a fitted kitchen that looked as if it had never been used, a gorgeous bathroom that was almost as good as the one at the *palácio*, and one bedroom—with a very large double bed and lots of mirrors.

Closing the door of the bedroom, she said stiffly, 'Is this where you bring all your women?'

Chris's mouth tightened a little and he said, 'Do you have a problem with that?'

Her eyes came up to meet his, prepared to challenge, but then she realised that she had forfeited the right to do so, and looked away, slowly shaking her head.

Taking out his wallet, Chris took out several notes and gave them to her. 'There isn't any food here. Take a taxi and go out and buy yourself a meal. Tomorrow morning I'll open accounts for you at some dress shops. Do you know which ones you want to use?'

Tiffany told him some names, the most expensive places she could think of, and added a beauty salon to the list. Chris noted them down without turning a hair.

'OK. I'd better be getting back. Will you be all right for now?'

'Yes.' She licked lips gone dry. 'And—later?'

Chris looked at her for a moment, then reached out and put his hand on her neck, let his thumb run along the line of her jaw. His eyes grew intent as he said, 'There's only one thing I want from you tonight.'

He waited, but she didn't answer, couldn't, her heart beginning to beat with nervous tension as she stood and stared at him, her eyes huge in her pale face. And what was the point anyway? They both knew what she was here for.

But then Chris amazed her for the second time that night by giving a small laugh as he took his hand away and held it out to her. 'Your passport.'

She stared. 'My—my what?'

'I want your passport.'

For a moment she didn't understand, but then it came to her; he was making sure she didn't just take his money and run, get on a train back to England or something. He obviously didn't trust her. But then, why should he? She had tricked her way into his life, so why shouldn't she trick her way out of it again?

'Of course,' she said stiffly, and took it out of her bag to hand it to him.

Chris flipped it open, read the details inside, but didn't comment, just stuffed the passport in his jacket pocket. Walking over to the phone, he took a note of the number, then said, 'I'll call you tomorrow and let you know when the accounts are open.' Going to the door, he opened it and looked back. 'Have a good meal and get some sleep. Goodnight, Tiffany.'

'Goodnight.' She stood there with open puzzlement in her face, having expected him at least to kiss her, to make some acknowledgement of their new relationship. Chris gave that small smile again, dropped the keys on the hall table, then left.

Glancing at her watch, Tiffany saw that only an hour and a half had passed since she had called him. The course of her life had changed in just that short time— and especially her surroundings. Tiffany put the chain on the door, then headed for the bathroom, shedding clothes as she went. Within minutes she was under the shower, scrubbing at her skin, washing her hair three times over. She hated not being clean, so not being able to have a bath or shower during these last few days had been the hardest thing of all to bear, worse than hunger, far worse than sleepless nights.

When her hair was dry, she counted the money Chris had given her. If she forgot about the food, there was enough for her train fare down to Lisbon, even down to the Algarve, where there might be a better chance of a job. But if not she would be in the same position as before. However, it wasn't that point that made her decide to stay; it was because Chris didn't trust her. Well, she didn't trust him either, not by a long way. But if she showed that she could keep her word, then that made her better than him, despite the circumstances.

So she called a taxi, had a meal in a good restaurant, then called another taxi to take her to an all-night shop where she bought make-up, tooth stuff and an unglamorous nightdress. Then she went back to the apartment, fell into bed and slept until the phone rang the next morning.

She roused herself reluctantly, but came quickly to her senses when she realised where she was. 'Hello?'

'Good morning.' There was a note of amusement in Chris's voice at the caution in her tone. 'I take it you slept well?'

'Like a dozen logs.'

'I've opened the accounts for you. You can go any time.'

'And the ball tonight?'

'What about it?'

'Have—have you got me an invitation?'

'You don't need an invitation; I can take whomever I please. But if what you're really saying is have I told

Calum and Francesca you're coming, then the answer's no.'

'I—I see.'

'No, you don't—and no more do I,' Chris said shortly. 'I'll pick you up at eight-thirty.'

Tiffany spent the whole day shopping, and being pampered in the beauty salon. She had a sauna, massage, manicure and pedicure, her hair done, the works. It cost a lot, but so what? She was a kept woman now, so let Chris keep her. After all, she thought with bitter irony, it was all for his benefit.

She bought a beautiful dress to wear that night. It was a pale gold colour with a long, straight satin skirt and a lacy top that came down to her hips and was hung with hundreds of drop beads. High heels made her taller and she had long gloves in the same colour as the dress. She looked cool and sophisticated—and very, very expensive.

When she opened the door to Chris that evening his eyes widened and he stood for a long moment, drinking her in. 'You look...' He came to a stop.

Tiffany had known that where Chris was concerned tonight was going to be difficult. After all, she had no experience of how to behave with a man who was about to take her as his kept mistress. She had decided to be pleasant but detached, so now she said, 'Aren't you going to finish?'

He shook his head. 'No, I don't think I am.'

Despite her resolution, she laughed. 'Now how am I supposed to take that?'

Chris grinned. 'Maybe I'll tell you some other time.' He held out his arm. 'Come on, Cinderella, let's go to the ball.'

CHAPTER FOUR

IT DIDN'T take long to reach the hotel where the ball was being held. There was a long line of cars waiting to park or drop their passengers, but Chris ducked round them into a reserved space.

They walked together into the hotel and Chris put a hand under her elbow as they walked up the steps, but it was merely a politeness and he took his hand away immediately afterwards. There were still several guests making their way to the ballroom, most of whom knew Chris. He said hello to them and walked on but one couple, just as they neared the ballroom, stopped him to compliment him on the wonderful week of festivities. Chris had to listen and thank them, and Tiffany moved on a few steps alone.

She could see into the ballroom where Chris's grandfather stood to greet his guests. Beside him was his daughter, Francesca's mother, and on her other side Calum was shaking hands with the latest arrivals. Beyond them the guests mingled, the hubbub of their voices drowning the band that played softly in the background. No one was dancing yet; the guests were too busy greeting friends, being handed drinks, and finding their allotted tables. There was a little hiatus as the people Calum had been talking to moved on, but the next couple had not yet reached him. He glanced towards them, then on to the door—and saw Tiffany.

For a moment he froze, then he strode forward and into the ante-room. Coming up to her, he took hold of Tiffany's arm and pulled her to the side of the room.

'How *dare* you come here? Do you really think you can pull off another stunt like the last one?' he demanded, his voice low and furious. His grip tightening, he said, 'I'm walking you out of here and I'm going to make darn sure you don't try to come back.'

He turned towards the entrance, but Chris had seen and came quickly over to them. 'Let her go, Calum.'

'What? Don't you know who——?'

'Tiffany is with me,' Chris said steadily.

His cousin stared at him. '*With* you?' The emphasis on the word made his meaning quite plain.

'Yes.'

Calum gave an involuntary gasp, then lowered his voice again to say forcefully, 'Are you mad? You can't know what you're letting yourself in for. And you certainly can't bring her here!'

'Well, I have brought her here—and what I do is my business, not yours—cousin. So take your damned hand off her.'

For a moment the two glared at each other, then Calum straightened up and shrugged. 'You'll regret this, Chris. She'll bring you nothing but trouble.'

'Some guests are waiting to shake your hand,' Chris pointed out grimly.

Calum gave him a baffled look, but turned and went back into the ballroom.

Tiffany slowly let out her breath and raised her eyes to look at Chris. There was a tight look to his features and the glance he gave her wasn't a pleasant one. 'Is that what you wanted?' he asked curtly. 'For us to quarrel over you?'

'No.' She shook her head, a rather sad look in her eyes. 'Families are precious; I'd never want you to be at odds with anyone you cared for.' Lifting her chin, she said, 'Let's go in, shall we?'

Chris gave her a puzzled look and shook his head, as if he didn't understand her. Not that Tiffany really understood herself, not right now.

They walked into the ballroom together and were received by Chris's grandfather, who greeted her with a warm smile and said it was nice to see her again. Francesca's mother, too, was charming, but Calum gave Tiffany a look of cold anger and didn't attempt to shake hands. Francesca, standing near by, saw Tiffany and her eyes widened, first in amazement and then in abhorrence. Tiffany put her hand on Chris's arm and gave the other girl a dazzling smile as they walked past, but then a great surge of intense bitterness suddenly filled her, a feeling so overwhelming that she couldn't bear it and had to fight it down. It took so much effort that it left her feeling drained and empty. But into the emptiness crept hatred and a desire to hurt as she was being hurt, to humiliate as she had been humiliated. That was a much harder emotion to conquer, and Tiffany didn't entirely succeed, but she took the glass of champagne that Chris handed to her and thought grimly, To hell with them; to hell with everything!

'What shall we drink to?' she asked, her eyes glittering with turbulent inner emotions.

'Suppose you tell me,' Chris answered, looking at her intently, a frown between his eyes.

Lifting the delicate glass high, Tiffany tilted her head, watching the bubbles pop. 'Let's drink to—drink,' she said on a note of caprice. 'To champagne that takes the pain away. To gin that makes your head spin. To whisky that makes you frisky.' She laughed on an unsteady note. 'And, most important, of course, to the port wine that has made your family rich.' Clinking her glass against Chris's, she raised it to her lips and drained it. Then, impatiently, she took his glass from him and set both of them down on a convenient table. 'Come on.' She pulled him towards the dance-floor. 'I want to dance until my feet wear out.'

From that moment she was very vivacious, bright and sparkling, so that anyone looking at her would have thought her very happy, without a care in the world and having a wonderful time. She swept round the floor in Chris's arms, drank more champagne, talked animatedly and laughed a lot. Only when she came face to face with Sam Gallagher did her brittle animation desert her. Tiffany happened to be alone for a moment, Chris having gone to the men's room, when Sam went to walk past her, stopped and stared, then came over.

'What are you doing here?' he demanded.

'I could ask you the same thing,' Tiffany countered.

'I was sent an invitation. How about you? Somehow I don't see you getting an invite after what happened.'

Tiffany gave a small smile. 'No, I didn't get an invitation. I—er—bought my way in.'

'Bought?' His brows drew into a frown.

'Figure it out,' she said lightly. 'I thought you'd had a row with Francesca?'

'I told her what I thought of her,' he admitted. Lifting his head, he looked across the ballroom to where Francesca was standing with the Count. 'That girl needs straightening out.'

'By a man?' Tiffany said, following his gaze. 'I hardly think Michel is the one to do it; Francesca has him under her elegant thumb.'

'Maybe you're right at that.' He looked thoughtful for a moment, but then his eyes came back to her as the band started to play a new number and he said casually, 'You care to dance?'

Tiffany shrugged and said, just as casually, 'OK.' Chris's reaction if he found her with another man did not even cross her mind.

It was a slow dance, and Tiffany rested her hand lightly on Sam's shoulder. For a moment she dropped the animated act, let herself just float, tried not to think of the future or the past, not to think of anything.

But Sam's voice saying, 'You didn't tell me how you come to be here,' intruded. He glanced down at her dress. 'And looking like a million dollars, too.'

For a moment it occurred to Tiffany to tell him the whole sorry story, and to beg him to help her. He might. He might lend her enough money to get to England, enough to find herself somewhere to live and get a job and . . . But then Tiffany remembered that Chris had her passport. The sudden spurt of hope died even more quickly than it had come. And anyway, what right had she to ask Sam to help her? None. All she had done was cause him embarrassment, first at the garden party and then at the *palácio* when Francesca had denounced her. All things considered it was a marvel he was even speaking to her. So she merely gave a shrug and said, 'Oh, I persuaded someone to bring me.'

Glancing across the room, she saw that Chris had come back and was looking round for her. Abandoning the Count, Francesca hurried over to him and began to speak to him heatedly. It didn't take much to guess what she was saying, especially when she gestured towards where Tiffany and Sam were dancing. Chris looked in their direction and his face hardened. Taking hold of Francesca, he pulled her on to the dance-floor and very deliberately moved in their direction.

Seeing Francesca immediately made Tiffany become very animated again, and she was laughing up at Sam

and he was smiling in amusement by the time Chris pro-
pelled Francesca up to them.

Reaching out, Chris put a hand on Sam's arm. 'Let's
exchange partners, shall we?'

Francesca opened her mouth to protest, but found
herself abandoned as Chris pulled Tiffany away.

For a moment he didn't speak, but then looked down
at her with cold anger in his eyes. 'Trying to get a better
offer?' he demanded sardonically.

Tiffany's instinctive reaction was to pull away from
him, but he had a firm grip on her hand and waist and
immediately pulled her back. 'You know something?'
she said tightly. 'You and Calum are very much alike.'

'I gather that isn't a compliment.'

'You're right, it isn't.'

His jaw tightened for a moment, but then Chris said,
'Yes, I suppose there are some ways in which we're alike.
For instance, we both hold on to what is ours.'

'Meaning?'

'Meaning that you and I made a bargain—and I'm
going to make darn sure that you keep it.' Pulling her
hard against him so that she could feel the powerfulness
of his body, he put his hand on her neck, his thumb
against her throat. 'So don't get any ideas about ducking
out. Wherever you ran to, I'd find you and bring you
back. You're mine, Tiffany. And you're going to stay
that way.' He paused, then added deliberately, 'Until, as
we agreed, I grow tired of you and let you go.'

She stared at him, overwhelmed by his sheer masculine strength, lost beneath his ruthless determination.
For the first time it really struck home that she had sold
herself to this man and was at his mercy, just as surely
as some slave in an ancient market-place. 'You—you'd
come after me?' she said on a low, unsteady note.

'You can bet your life on it. Like Calum, I make sure
I keep my possessions.'

Tiffany had nothing to say to that. She turned her
head away, looked blindly across the ballroom. I
shouldn't have come here, she thought. It was a mistake.
I don't belong here, among these rich, selfish people.
She knew now that by making Chris bring her she had
been trying to prove to herself that she was as good as
the Brodeys, that she had as much right to be here as
any of the guests. But she had found just the opposite.
Pride deserted her and she felt desolate. But then that
feeling of hatred for the Brodeys came back, this time
far more forcefully. And this time she didn't fight it but
instead fed on it, so that her chin came up and she gave
Chris a smile in which coldness glittered like ice.

'How long does it usually take you before you tire of
your women?' she asked with sardonic flippancy. 'Just
on average will do. You don't have to be specific.'

'What kind of question is that?' Chris said roughly.

'I'm just trying to find out how long I'm likely to be
your—"possession".'

The music came to an end and Chris stood still. There
was a strange glint in his eyes as he stood looking down
at her. 'Well, now, that might take some time. After all,
you did promise to be anything I wanted you to be.'

Tiffany stared at him wide-eyed, feeling suddenly
afraid, like a small child faced with something it didn't
understand. Her lips parted but she couldn't speak.

The look in Chris's eyes changed, darkened with
desire. Putting a hand on her arm, he said, thickly, 'Let's
get out of here.'

They went back to the flat and had sex. There was no
way you could call it making love.

Chris had walked her out of the ball, not bothering to say goodnight to any of his family. They had got into his car and he had driven fast and silently back into town to the apartment building. He had remained silent while he'd taken her up in the lift, into the flat and on into the bedroom. He'd snapped on a couple of lamps, drawn the curtains, then turned and spoke for the first time. 'Now show me what I've bought.'

Tiffany stared at him, realising what he wanted. She was already taut with nervous tension, but now her heart began to beat wildly in her chest. I can't do this, she thought in panic. I can't! Her eyes went to Chris, looking for compassion, but he was watching her intently, his features sharpened by erotic anticipation, that strange, dark look in his eyes again. What she saw drained all hope from her. There was no way he was going to take a denial. And why should he? They had made a bargain which he had kept, and now she must pay the price.

Deliberately she cut out Chris and her surroundings, thought only of the squalor of the house where she'd lived last, of being dirty and hungry. Trying desperately to keep only those things in her mind, she lifted her hands to the button at the back of her dress and began to take off her clothes.

Chris stood and watched her as she took off the garments one by one and let them drop to the floor. Her top and skirt, the gloves, a long silk slip that came almost down to her feet. His hands were thrust into his trouser pockets and he must have clenched them, because the material became taut across his hips. Tiffany stepped out of her shoes, bent to remove her pale stockings, and was unable to cut herself off any longer. Her emotions were here and now, raw and chaotic. Straightening, she saw the deep hunger in Chris's eyes, the tiny beads of sweat on his upper lip, and the growing hardness of his body.

She became still, and he said impatiently, roughly, '*Go on.*'

She shook her head. 'No, damn you. I won't!'

His eyes came up to meet hers. 'Anything I want you to be,' he reminded her thickly.

His gaze seemed to drain the defiance from her. Slowly she took off her underwear and let the wisps of silk and lace fall from her fingers.

Only then did he cross to her, touch her. Tiffany shut her eyes, not wanting to see, trying to detach her mind from her body. At first his fingers seemed unsure, unsteady, touching her lightly, but each touch leaving a trail of heat across her skin. Gradually his hands became more sure as he explored her, and it was hard just to stand passively and let him do what he wanted.

He moved away, came back, came close. Deliberately he moved his leg against hers and she felt the silkiness of his bare skin. He bent and she felt his lips on her breast. Tiffany gave an involuntary gasp, hastily cut short. She felt him grow still for a moment, but she kept her eyes tight shut, stood stiff and unyielding before him. He began to caress her again and his hands were urgent now, trembling with inordinate desire as he held and stroked her. And they were so hot, so hot. She had to stifle a quiver of emotion, kill the awakening awareness in her own body. His breath was hoarse now, panting. Suddenly Chris swept her up in his arms and carried her to the bed, lowered her on to it and came over her all in one movement.

Opening her eyes, she saw him above her, his face dark with sexual need. Lifting a hand, he put it against her face. Tiffany jerked away and, her eyes burning into his, said with fierce loathing, 'I *hate* you.'

For a brief second he checked, and his brows flickered, but then he gave an odd, grim kind of laugh and said, 'Well, that's novel.' But then he came down on her and said through gritted teeth, 'But let's see if you hate this.'

She didn't hate it, and was ashamed of herself for not doing so. She tried to be stiff and detached, to think only of how much she hated Chris and all the Brodeys, but somewhere along the line her errant body betrayed her, and she found herself moving to accept him, her hands lifting to grip his shoulders, and her mouth opening to moan with pleasure.

Afterwards, when Chris had groaned out his own excitement and moved away from her, he put a possessive arm across her and lowered his head to kiss her. But by then waves of shame at her own lack of will-power had hit her and Tiffany was close to tears. Pushing him away, she rolled off the bed and ran into the bathroom, locking the door behind her. Leaning against the door, she stood in trembling agitation, her hands gripped together and pressed against her mouth, stifling the sobs so that he wouldn't hear. But they were more sobs of rage at herself than of distress. Why couldn't she have controlled her stupid body? Why?

Because it had been good, that was why. The reason was simple enough. Chris's reputation with women had not been an idle one; he knew how to please a woman and lift her to the heights. How to make love. No, not make love, how to have sex skilfully. Love didn't come into it, and it was a word she would never think of in connection with him, with the act they had just performed.

Act. That word stayed in her mind as Tiffany stood under the shower and turned on the water. If she could pretend that this wasn't real, that she was just an actress playing a part, maybe that would help her to be de-

tached from it. But she still despised herself for having
found pleasure in it when Chris had merely been using
her for his own gratification. Why did it always have to
be that way? Why couldn't women use men for *their*
pleasure? That's what I'd like to do, she thought, show
him what it's like to be used. Make him feel the way I'm
feeling now. But that was just a fantasy, a wishful dream
born of her own guilt and shame which was soon pushed
to the back of her mind.

But the idea about acting a part stayed in her mind,
helped somehow.

Tiffany dried herself off and put on the new bathrobe
that she had bought that morning. When she came out
into the bedroom she found that Chris had got into the
bed and was asleep. She found a black silk nightdress
and put it on, then turned towards the bed, but hesitated.

As she gazed down at Chris it came to her that she
had never really looked at him before. When they had
first met her attention had been solely on Calum, and
since then the only times she'd seen Chris seemed to have
been too charged with tension for her really to register
how he looked. But now, while he slept, she studied his
face, thinking that, although he resembled his male
cousins in some ways, Chris was the least typical of the
Brodeys. Whereas they were blond, Chris's hair,
probably because of his half-Portuguese mother, was
brown, and there was a hint of his high-bred Latin
ancestors in the clean angles of his cheeks and jawbone
and in his high forehead. But the passionate line of his
mouth, the long lashes that brushed his cheeks, his tall,
muscular body, they were all from his father, from his
Brodey blood.

His eyes opened and he looked directly at her as she
stood over him. He didn't blink or look startled, just let
his eyes travel over her and take in the black négligé that

clung to her body, revealing nothing and yet hiding nothing. When she didn't speak, he sat up and said, 'So you didn't hate it.'

There was no point in denying it; it had been plain enough to them both. Her chin came up. 'So?'

Holding out his hand to her, his voice silky, Chris said, 'So come back to bed.'

Tiffany hesitated, trying to think herself into a part, an actress's role, but she hesitated too long. With a low chuckle, Chris reached for her hand and pulled her down beside him.

A third time that night, and again in the morning, he took her. And although it was the same, each time was somehow different. Perhaps it was the tempo. That first time Chris had been driven by an overwhelming sexual need which was hardly slaked after the second and third times, but in the morning he woke before her and it was the touch of his lips on her breasts that brought her back to awareness, not only of her surroundings, but of the sexual arousal of her own body. He put his hand on her hip, let it stroke down her leg, but he was intent on what he was doing, not caring whether she was awake or not. But it was impossible to feign sleep when her breasts hardened under his mouth, when he rained kisses up the column of her throat and along her chin. He came to her mouth, which was parted in breathless sensuality, and hovered there for a moment, his eyes dark and heavy with his own heated desire.

Lowering his head, he went to kiss her lips, but Tiffany turned her head away. Immediately he put his hand under her chin and forced her head back, even though she tried her best to resist him. She glared up at him defiantly, and he lowered his head again. But he didn't kiss her properly, merely brushed her lips lightly with his, then looked at her mockingly, letting her know that he could have done if he'd wanted to, if he'd cared enough to force the issue. But he didn't. Why should he when he could take the rest of her whenever he pleased? Like now. He put a hand under her and arched her towards him, the better for her small, delicate body to accommodate his dominant masculinity, then he took her with slow, unhurried strokes that nevertheless brought her again to the heights of sexual excitement.

They both showered, Chris wrapping a white bathsheet round himself afterwards as he went into the kitchen to look for something to eat.

'Hey, didn't you buy any food?' he called out.

Tiffany came out of the bathroom, doing up the belt of her robe. 'No.' She noticed there were red marks on his shoulders where her fingers had gripped him.

'Why not?'

She shrugged. 'There wasn't time yesterday. And anyway...'

Chris straightened up from looking in the fridge. 'Yes?'

It was difficult to put what she wanted to say into words. Tiffany wasn't even sure that she wanted to tell him that yesterday she had given no thought to today, that she hadn't even wanted to think about it. 'I just didn't get round to it,' she said, because he was waiting.

'We'd better go out for some breakfast, then.'

'I'm not hungry.' She didn't want to go out. She was mentally and physically exhausted from the night before.

'You're not? I'm starving; I need to go out and eat.'

'In the evening clothes you were wearing last night?'

'Oh, yeah, I forgot.' Going into the bedroom, Chris picked up his trousers and took his car keys from the pocket. 'I brought a bag with me but I left it in the car. Why don't you dress and then go and bring it up for me?'

Chris had couched it as a request but really, of course, it was an instruction. He lay down on the bed again, propped up on his elbow, while Tiffany sorted out some clothes. She started to carry them to the bathroom to dress, but Chris said, 'No. Do it in here.'

She was still for a moment, but then her features became set as she obeyed him. Very conscious of his eyes on her, she wondered if he expected her to make a show of it, like a strip-tease in reverse, like last night in reverse. If so, he was disappointed. Shutting him out as much as she could, she just got dressed in the normal way, as she always did.

Glancing past her reflection in the mirror as she put on her make-up, she noticed that Chris again had that odd sort of hooded look in his eyes. She couldn't fathom it, didn't even much care. Ready now, she turned to face him. 'Is that how you get your kicks?' she asked him. 'Watching women dress and undress?'

His brows flickered, but he said, 'That's right. I can't get enough of it.'

Disgust showed in her eyes and voice as Tiffany said, 'I bet you read porno magazines too.'

His mouth quirked mockingly. 'Why should I—when I have the real thing right here?'

She had left herself wide open to that one, she realised. Picking up the keys, she let herself out of the flat and leaned back in the empty lift with her eyes closed. She had got over the worst, she told herself. After last night it would just be repetition. Maybe Chris would soon grow tired of her. But he was so virile; she hadn't expected that. But then, he was still young, only about thirty, if not younger. For the first time it crossed her mind to wonder why, when he had such a reputation and was still young, he had bothered to make that bargain with her, why he had made her his mistress at all. With his

looks and his money, there must be any number of girls
that he could seduce, if not here, then in any of the
countries where he was a frequent visitor. And if Calum
Brodey was the most eligible bachelor around, then Chris
must be a close second.

Tiffany frowned, thinking that it didn't add up. Unless
of course Chris had been piqued because she had turned
him down originally, had made it plain from the start
that she wasn't interested, so that he had been determined to get her, even to buy her if it was necessary.
Yes, that was far more likely. That added up all right.
And she was more convinced than ever now that it had
been Chris who'd told Francesca that she was a gatecrasher in their fairy-tale palace, in their synthetic lives.

She got his bag from the car and after she gave it to
him Chris dressed, but she didn't watch him. He'd
brought well-cut casual clothes that didn't look out of
place in the tourist hotel where he took her for breakfast.
It was a few miles along the coast, a place where he
evidently wasn't known. He had stopped to buy a paper
on the way and read the financial section as he ate.
Tiffany didn't mind; she wasn't exactly the talkative type
first thing in the morning herself. Finishing first, she sat
back and wondered what she was supposed to do for
the rest of the day. Would Chris leave her at the flat
while he went back to the *palácio*, or what? She had
thought before that she had no future; now she didn't
even know what was going to happen even an hour into
the future.

The thought made her give a twisted smile of irony,
which Chris, glancing up, noticed. 'What is it?'

Remembrance of the night came to her and she said,
'I feel like an actor waiting for the director to tell me
what to do; that I have no mind of my own and must
wait until the script is ready and I'm given instructions.'

His eyes stayed on her face. 'And am I the director?'

'Yes.' Her voice grew bitter. 'The puppeteer pulling the strings of the marionette.'

'Marionettes are made of wood.'

'Yes, I know.'

Leaning forward, Chris's voice suddenly became intense. 'You're not made of wood, Tiffany. You proved that last night. And, no matter how you try to hold back, you'll never be able to. Because you're too sensuous by nature.' He gave her a knowing grin. 'Because you like it too darn much.'

She stared at him, feeling annihilated by shame, a shame that quickly turned to anger. 'I hate you,' she told him for the second time.

Chris laughed. 'No, you don't. You just hate the way I make you feel. You were all set to lie there like some martyr, as stiff as a stone, but you found you couldn't, and that's what's making you angry. Not me.'

'You're completely wrong,' Tiffany said shortly. 'I do hate you—and all your family.'

But Chris wasn't in the least put out. Glancing at his watch, he said, 'Talking of family, I suppose I'd better be getting back to the house. We're having a last lunch, all of us together, before everyone starts to leave.'

'Aren't you going to take me with you?' Tiffany said provocatively.

'Not this time. Family only.' Chris folded his paper and stood up.

'Then don't go. Stay with me.' Getting to her feet, she moved to stand close to him, and leaned her shoulder against him in a small but intimate gesture.

It was a test of power she knew she didn't have. Not now he'd taken her. He'd wanted her enough to agree to take her to the ball, but he would never allow her to encroach again.

His eyes smiled a little and he put a hand on her shoulder in a possessive gesture, but he shook his head. 'My parents are leaving to go back to Lisbon after lunch, and I must be there to say goodbye to them.' They walked out to the car, his hand still on her shoulder. 'I'll drop you in town. Buy some food, enough for about three days. Can you cook?'

'No,' Tiffany lied.

Chris grinned. 'Somehow I didn't think you could. Just get breakfast stuff, then, and we'll eat out in the evenings.'

'And after three days?'

'Oh, yes, buy a suitcase. We'll be moving on.'

'Where to?'

'New York first, then around.'

'Around where?'

'Wherever I have to go on company business.'

He said it vaguely. Perhaps he meant to. It certainly didn't make Tiffany feel any more secure, give her much future to look forward to. But the thought of going to America pleased and excited her; she would be glad to leave Portugal behind; nothing good had happened to her here. Except meeting Isabel and the girls; their friendship and kindness had made up for a lot. Thinking of them made her say to Chris as he drove along, 'I shall need some more money.'

Leaning forward, he fished his wallet out of his pocket and handed it to her. 'Take what you want out of there.'

The gesture surprised her; she hadn't expected him to be so open, so generous. But maybe he felt sure of her now, convinced that she wouldn't try to run out on him. Because of the money—or because she'd enjoyed the sex? That last thought was pushed hastily out of her mind. Flipping open the wallet, she took out some notes. There were other things in there, credit cards, that kind of thing, but she didn't notice any photographs. She gave him back the wallet and put the money in her purse.

When he dropped her in the Praca da Republica, the first thing she did was phone the girls and invite them out to lunch. 'My treat,' she told them. 'And I hope you're hungry.'

There were hugs all round when they met, and they had a great lunch at one of the best restaurants in Oporto, drinking wine and laughing a lot. The girls were tactful, not asking where the money for the meal or for Tiffany's new clothes had come from. But then they didn't have to; they had already guessed. Afterwards Tiffany gave each of them a present of a box of exquisite lingerie that she had charged to Chris's account. But when the others had gone and the time came to say goodbye to Isabel, the Portuguese girl gave her a troubled look.

'Are you happy with what you are doing?'

'Sure. Of course.' Tiffany made her voice as positive as she possibly could.

'This man,' Isabel said hesitantly. 'Is he the one who came looking for you at our boarding house after you had left? Did he find you?'

'Came looking for me?' Tiffany frowned. 'But no one knew I was there. Did you see this man? What did he look like?'

'No, I was at work. But Senhora Mota who lives on the first floor, she saw the man and heard 'im talking to the landlord, and she told us. She said he was not Portuguese, although he spoke the language perfectly. That he was tall and looked English or American. She said his clothes were good. Does that help? Is it 'im?'

'Yes,' Tiffany said thoughtfully. 'That does sound like him.'

'Senhora Mota said he was very 'andsome,' Isabel said
on a note of curiosity. 'Perhaps you are in love with 'im,
no?'

'No,' Tiffany said definitely, but then quickly put a
reassuring hand on Isabel's arm as she saw the disappointment in her face. 'But the *senhora* is right; he is
quite good-looking.'

'So perhaps you will fall in love soon,' Isabel smiled.

She had to rush away then, to go back to work, and
Tiffany watched her go with regret; it was hardly likely
that they would ever meet again. Turning away, her face
hardened. It was clear that Chris had found out where
she was living, so it could only have been he who had
told the landlord about her and got her turned out. He
must have known that she was near enough destitute and
was hardly likely to get a job. All he'd had to do then
was wait until she got desperate enough to call him. No
wonder it had taken him so little time to arrange the
apartment for her; he must have had it all ready and
waiting. '"Come into my parlour," said the spider to
the fly.' The aptness of the quotation made her rage inwardly. How easily she had fallen into the trap that Chris
had set for her. What a gullible fool! She ought to have
realised it could only have been him.

Again she thought of walking out on him, and,
turning, began to stride towards the station, seething with
anger. OK, so she couldn't leave Portugal because Chris
had her passport, but she could go to Lisbon, hide herself
away there. But just as she was entering the building she
stopped suddenly. Chris had said that he would come
after her, bring her back. And he could do it, too. He
had power here, where she had none. She couldn't hide
away for long; she would have to come out to look for
work, and then he would surely find her and drag her
ignominiously back. And then where would her pride—

all that she had left—be? A sense of fatalism swept over her, and she slowly turned to retrace her steps. But the knowledge of the dirty trick Chris had played on her had added fuel to the hatred growing inside her.

She bought the food that Chris had instructed her to get, just buying the minimum necessary, then took a cab back to the apartment. A maid must have been in: the bed was made and there were fresh towels in the bathroom. Suddenly she felt dreadfully tired, and after putting the food away she took off her dress and shoes and lay on the bed to rest. Sunlight lay across her, making her feel warm, so that she didn't cover herself. The sleepless night and the wine she had drunk at lunchtime sent her quickly and deeply into slumber, and she didn't hear the door open an hour or so later as Chris came into the room.

It was his shadow lying across her, cutting off the light and warmth of the sun, that brought her back to consciousness. He was standing over her, watching her as she slept, making her feel vulnerable. She went to sit up, but he lay down quickly beside her and put a hand on her shoulder to push her down again. 'No,' he said in a voice charged with need. 'Stay right there where you belong.'

'No, I don't want to.' She went to hit out at him but he caught her wrists, and held them against the pillow above her head with one hand.

He laughed softly. Unhooking her bra, he began to caress her with his free hand and his mouth. His lips lit deep, consuming fires within her that betrayed her resolution, killed all resistance. 'Don't you?' he breathed, his lips against her throat. 'Do you really want me to stop?'

'Yes.'

His hand immediately became still and he drew back, letting her go.

For a moment she stared up at him, but then gave a low sob and said, 'No!' And, reaching out, she pulled him down again.

CHAPTER FIVE

TIFFANY had forgotten to buy a suitcase. Next day when she woke she found Chris gone, but there was a note saying that he would be back that evening to take her out to dinner. So all she had to do, for the next ten hours, was to buy the suitcase. It came to her that mistresses must spend most of their time just waiting around for their lovers, making sure they were beautiful and available whenever the men had time for them. Enough women did it and were probably happy, but Tiffany found the life completely alien to her.

I'm just not used to being a rich man's plaything, she thought sardonically as she showered.

She dressed quickly, avoiding looking at the tumbled bed, trying to put all thoughts of the hours they'd spent in it yesterday afternoon, and again in the night, out of her mind. Which wasn't easy when she was reluctantly recognising that her body was not only getting used to the pleasure that Chris's skill constantly gave her, but was rapidly becoming eager for more. That soon she would need him as much as he seemed to need her. Until he grew tired of her and kicked her out.

Grimly, Tiffany let herself out of the flat and took the tram into town, then walked round to look at the boarding house where she'd lived with the girls, deliberately reminding herself of who she really was.

After a while she turned and walked back to the city centre, to a shop where she bought the most expensive set of matching luggage that she could find. She ordered it to be sent round to the apartment, then went to find a café for some lunch. As she crossed the road she almost bumped into Sam Gallagher who was crossing the other way.

'Tiffany! Hey, hello,' Sam said surprised.

'Hello, Sam. How are you?'

'Great. How about you?'

The lights changed, cars began to hoot, and for a moment they stood undecided in the middle of the road, but then Sam turned and hurried to the pavement with her.

'A girl could get killed talking to you,' Tiffany said laughingly.

He grinned back and said, 'You're looking pretty good.'

'Am I?' There was surprise in her voice until she remembered that she was wearing a very expensive outfit. 'Oh, you mean the clothes. Thanks.'

'No, that isn't what I meant. You look . . .' He paused, then gave a small laugh. 'Perhaps I'd better not say how you look. Are you going somewhere special?'

'Just to find a café for lunch.'

'How about joining me?'

'Thank you; I'd like to.'

They started to walk along the street, and Sam said, 'You sure you're not meeting Chris?'

'What difference would that make?'

'He's the jealous type; I wouldn't want to get my nose punched.'

Tiffany smiled, looking at his broad shoulders. 'I think you could take care of yourself.'

He led her along, seeming to know where he was going, till they came to one of the best-known restaurants in town, a *churrasquiera*, where they specialised in chicken dishes cooked the Portuguese way. Sam spoke to the head waiter and they were led to a table by the wall, where a huge mirror gave extra dimension to the room. Sam sat against the wall so that Tiffany had her back to the room.

'How much longer are you going to be in Portugal? I thought your holiday would be finished by now,' Tiffany remarked.

'I thought I'd stay on a while,' he answered casually. 'Let's have a drink first, shall we? What would you like?'

'Gin and tonic, please.'

They ordered then Sam said, 'What have you been doing since the ball?' He raised a questioning eyebrow. 'Or shouldn't I ask that?'

As Tiffany seemed to have spent most of the time in bed with Chris, she naturally coloured a little, and said, 'Maybe it would be better if you didn't.'

'Are you and Chris an item?'

'We've only known each other a short time,' she prevaricated, not wanting to reveal the true situation.

'Yeah, but I thought, back at the Brodeys' place, that day after the garden party, that he was gone on you.'

Tiffany shook her head, a puzzled look in her eyes. 'Oh, I don't think so.'

'Sure he was. If I hadn't torn Francesca off a strip he would have done it instead.'

There was a language problem here, Tiffany thought. When Sam said that Chris was 'gone' on her, he must mean that Chris had made it obvious that he fancied her, that was all.

'Oh, no, Chris and I are just—just friends, I suppose.' Which was a tactful lie for Sam's benefit. Intimate enemies was the true way she would have described their relationship.

The waiter came with their drinks. Glancing up, Tiffany chanced to look in the mirror—and froze. Francesca had come into the restaurant. The head waiter, recognising her, bowed deeply, Francesca smiled and spoke—and the waiter began to lead her in their direction!

'Sam,' Tiffany hissed, but he was asking the waiter's advice about the wine list and didn't hear.

Her forward vision impaired by the head waiter's back, Francesca nodded to some other diners that she knew and didn't notice Tiffany until the waiter moved aside and pulled out a chair for her. It was then that Sam saw her and, to Tiffany's stupefaction, merely stood up and said, 'Hi there, Francesca. Look who I ran into in town and asked to join us for lunch.'

Both girls stared at each other for a moment, Francesca in stunned surprise, but then her face froze with anger. Leaning towards Sam, she said in a low voice full of venom, 'If this is your idea of a joke, then you have an extremely warped sense of humour.'

She went to swing away, but Sam was near enough to catch her arm. Exerting his strength, he forced her into a seat, saying tersely, 'Sit down, Princess. Join the party.'

Francesca could have fought him off, could have called the waiter over, but she was fully aware of the gossip that would cause, so she gave him a killing look but stayed in the chair. Sam watched her for a moment, until he was sure of her, then let go of her wrist. 'What would you like to drink? Campari?'

Francesca didn't answer, just glared at him, but Sam calmly nodded at the hovering waiter.

When he'd gone, she said furiously, 'How dare you plan this?'

'I didn't plan it,' Sam answered. 'As I said, Tiffany and I ran into each other quite by accident.'

'Well, if you didn't plan it, then *she* certainly did. I doubt very much if she ever does anything "by accident".'

Tiffany leant forward angrily, 'Now just a minute——'

But Francesca, ignoring her, said to Sam, 'If you think I'm going to sit here with that—that—with *her*, then you're crazy!'

'And just why shouldn't you sit with Tiffany?' Sam's face hadn't changed but there was a note of menace in his voice that Tiffany caught.

But Francesca was too angry to notice. 'I should have thought that was obvious.'

'So she crashed your party. And you showed her up in front of your cousins. So that's it, quits. And I'll damn well ask who I want to lunch.'

'Not with me, you won't!' Francesca's voice had risen a little and people on the next table looked round. Quickly lowering it again, and still speaking to Sam as if Tiffany weren't there, she said, fiercely, 'Don't you know what she is? Do you really not know?'

Tiffany felt that she wanted to die. She gave Sam a look full of helpless anger. Why the hell couldn't he have told her he was meeting Francesca, then all this could have been avoided? She tried to interrupt, but there was no stopping Francesca now.

'She's no better than a prostitute. Don't you understand? She *sold* herself to Chris. Where else do you think she got the clothes she's wearing? How else would she have been able to go to our ball?'

'Before you ask,' Tiffany said to Sam bitterly as he went to speak, 'it's quite true.'

'I wasn't going to ask. And what the hell does it matter anyway?' Leaning forward, he grabbed Francesca's wrist as she went to rise in indignation. 'No, stay where you are. And now *you* listen,' he said to her, his voice like steel. 'Who the hell are you to judge Tiffany? Have you bothered to find out what drove her to do it? Any of

It? Can't you see that she's the kind of girl who would have to be desperate to do something like that? And so what if she has known other men? At least she doesn't go through the hypocrisy of marriage and divorce. And what if Chris has given her clothes and money? Didn't your Italian prince give you clothes and money when you sold yourself to him for the title?'

For a long moment there was a stunned silence at the table. Tiffany couldn't believe that Sam had said it, had dared to say it. Francesca, too, looked as if she had been punched in the jaw.

Into the electric silence the waiter innocently walked up with Francesca's Campari. 'Your drink, *senhora.*'

'*Obrigada.*' Picking up the drink, Francesca threw it in Sam's face.

He saw it coming a mile off and let go of her wrist as he jerked his head to one side, but a lot of it went over his suit. His eyes narrowing, he said in a voice of cold, silken menace, 'You'll pay for that one day, *Princess.*'

After what had gone before, the emphasis was a definite insult. Francesca rose to her full height, her face contemptuous. 'I'll leave you two together. You obviously deserve each other.' And she strode out of the restaurant.

Picking up his napkin, Sam calmly began to dab at his suit. 'Sorry about that.'

Tiffany let out her breath. 'I'm not surprised she threw it at you. I'd have done the same.'

He raised an eyebrow. 'What's this—feminine solidarity? I'd have thought you'd be on my side.'

'Well, I'm not. Why didn't you say that you were meeting Francesca? You know she can't stand me.'

'She ought to be more tolerant, more understanding.'

Incensed, Tiffany said, 'Is that why you invited me? Just so that you could see how Francesca would react? Was it all some kind of test for her?'

'No, it wasn't. I wanted to——'

He broke off as Tiffany, too, got to her feet and picked up her glass.

'Now wait a minute...' A wary look came into Sam's eyes.

'Oh, don't worry,' she said shortly. 'I wouldn't waste good booze.' Draining the glass, she set it down on the table. 'Enjoy your lunch, Sam.' And she too walked out of the restaurant.

Out in the street, Tiffany looked round and saw Francesca striding away, her back still rigid with anger. She made a movement as if to catch her, to tell her that she was just as annoyed with Sam, but then stopped; Francesca was too mad either to listen or care. And anyway, she had been unnecessarily rude; she hadn't needed to tell Sam the truth about her and Chris, although Tiffany was pretty sure that he already knew. She turned away, feeling once more that she had been used. Why Sam had done it she didn't know. But it certainly hadn't been planned as Francesca had said; she and Sam really had met quite by chance so he must have decided to use her on the spur of the moment. But then, she had done exactly the same thing to Sam at the garden party, she thought ruefully, and instead of being angry became intrigued as she wondered what Sam was up to.

When Chris came to collect her that evening, Tiffany immediately sensed that there was something wrong. He was polite enough, talked to her about nothing very much over dinner in a Chinese restaurant and, when they went back to the flat, immediately took her to bed. But afterwards, instead of lying back to rest, he got up and went over to his clothes.

'Are you leaving?' Tiffany asked in surprise.

He glanced over his shoulder at her. 'Why? Someone else you want to invite over?' he asked sarcastically.

Tiffany sat up, pulling the sheet up to cover her chest. 'What's that supposed to mean?'

'Are you playing around with Sam Gallagher? Doing a little overtime?'

Her face white, Tiffany said, 'I don't deserve that from you.'

'No?'

'No. I don't "play around" as you call it.'

Coming back to stand by the bed, Chris said with a short laugh, 'You're hardly in a position to make that kind of statement.'

Tiffany turned her face away, embarrassed by his nakedness. 'This is—different. As far as I'm concerned it's just a business arrangement. I've…contracted myself, I suppose you could call it, to you. And I'll keep my side of the bargain as long as you keep yours. And I *certainly* don't want anyone else.'

Chris gave her a speculative look. 'Why not? Sam's a good-looking man, attractive to women. And he's got money; he could pay.'

The eyes that turned to look at his face were dark with withering contempt. 'He's a man, isn't he?'

'Ouch!' Chris gave a mock-wince. Getting on to the bed, he leaned against the headboard and put his hands on her shoulders, began to massage them. 'So you're telling yourself you hate all men, are you?'

'Not just men; I don't exactly like Francesca either—spreading her poison around. Sam's right: she needs teaching a lesson.'

'Somehow I don't think she'll be seeing Sam again, not after today.' His hand left her shoulder and his fingers traced down her spine, right to its tip, his touch light, feathery, sensuous. 'You have a beautiful little body, Tiffany. Just made for love.'

Her voice a little unsteady, she said, 'This isn't love.'

Slipping his hands under her arms, he pulled down the sheet and cupped her breasts, stroked them tantalisingly. 'Ah, feminine shades of distinction. OK, so what would you call this?'

Trying not to show that he was getting to her, Tiffany said, 'Lust, of course. Just male gratification.'

'*Male* gratification?' He leaned her back against him so that he could watch what his hands were doing. 'Are you trying to tell me you don't get anything out of it?'

She was silent for a moment, knowing that her nipples were already aroused, that to deny it was impossible. 'I don't want to,' she said at last, her voice faltering on a sigh of awareness.

'No, but you can't help it.' He kissed her neck, the lobe of her ear, let his fingers tighten. 'You need a man to make you feel like this; you'll always need a man.'

Tiffany closed her eyes, wondering why, if what he said was true, no other man had ever made her feel like this before.

Suddenly he pulled her over so that she was lying on top of him. Gripping her arms, his eyes hard and threatening, Chris said forcefully, 'And just so long as I'm paying the bills, then I intend to be that man—the only one. Do you understand?' She stared down at him and he gave her an impatient shake. 'Well, do you?'

Feeling suddenly afraid, she said, 'Yes,' in a low, obedient voice.

'Good.' The sheet was between them. Reaching down, he pulled it clear. 'So why don't you keep your side of the bargain?'

* * *

Two days later they left Portugal and flew to New York. Tiffany hadn't been there before and found the city exciting, the pace entirely different from that of London and a world away from Oporto. Chris had an apartment in Manhattan, a bachelor pad with a tiny kitchen and a big circular bed—which figured. Tiffany had expected things to be as they were in Oporto: that Chris would leave her on her own during the day and come back at night. But he was different here. Tiffany sensed an easing of tension in him, and right from the start he took her out and about with him. Took her out of the cupboard and dusted her off, so to speak.

Brodey's had an office in New York, but Chris did a lot of his work from the flat, via the phone or his computer, and Tiffany found Chris Brodey, executive businessman, something of a revelation. He was very single-minded, very determined, willing to go to great lengths to get a sizeable order. He did a lot of research, too. If someone opened up a liquor store, Chris arranged for a complimentary vintage bottle of port to be sent. If Chris persuaded the owner of a chain of stores to stock Brodey's in favour of other ports, then Chris made sure that that person would receive a case of the best port at Christmas. And if he was a really good customer, then he received an invitation to visit the Brodey vineyards either in Portugal or Madeira. And Chris thought nothing of hiring a plane and flying anywhere in the States to get a good order.

And he took Tiffany with him. In the first two months they were there, Chris flew her to Texas, California, and over to Montana, introducing her quite calmly as 'my assistant, Tiffany Dean'. And when they were in New York he seemed to enjoy showing her the city, taking her to the tourist places and the theatre, as well as to a different restaurant every night. He even introduced her to his friends, which was something she definitely hadn't expected. But he made the position clear by putting a possessive hand on her shoulder or waist as he said merely, 'This is Tiffany.'

There were some women among those she met whom Tiffany was quite sure Chris had had affairs with in the past. It was in the way they looked at him and the smile he gave in return. And sometimes, too, in the way they looked at or spoke to Tiffany. Just small things that betrayed that they were jealous or envious, although one girl, who followed Tiffany into the ladies' room at a party, said quite openly, 'How did you manage to hook Chris? You're so lucky. He's a great lover.' The girl sighed. 'It's that European temperament, I suppose, and the lack of any inhibitions.'

'He was your lover, was he?' Tiffany felt emboldened to ask.

'Yes, for a while. But certainly not for long enough.'

'What happened? Why did you split up?'

'It just sort of faded out. Chris went away on one of his trips and when he came back he just didn't call me. He's still playing the field, I guess.' The girl pulled a rueful face. 'But I sure wish he'd picked up the phone, because I certainly hadn't had enough of *him*.'

Tiffany heard the jealousy in her voice with amusement, and wondered what the girl would have said if she'd known the true situation. Wondered too, for the hundredth time, why Chris was keeping her when he could choose from a selection of good-looking girls who all seemed to be eager for him, and for free, too. Whereas she made a point of asking whether he'd got tired of her yet, just to remind him that her body might be involved, but nothing else. But, strangely, it didn't do Tiffany's morale any harm to know that she was envied.

During that time Chris announced one day that he had to go to Chicago. He had been to the office and told her when he came back, standing in front of the mirror and knotting his tie, just before they went out to eat. Tiffany was sitting on the bed, putting on her shoes. To test him she said, 'Why don't you leave me here?'

His eyes left his own reflection to settle on hers. 'I want you with me,' he said brusquely.

'Why?'

His eyebrows flickered for a moment, but then he gave a short laugh. 'Why the hell do you think?'

Tiffany's face hardened and she didn't attempt to hide the antagonism in her eyes.

Turning, his tie knotted, Chris said shortly, 'What other answer did you expect?'

She gave a brittle smile and stood up. 'None, of course.' Walking ahead of him, she went out of the apartment and punched the button for the lift. When they were going down in it, she said, 'But don't I get any days off in this job?'

He looked amused. 'You ought to have negotiated those right at the beginning. As far as I'm concerned, it's a full-time occupation.'

She pouted moodily. 'I may go on strike.'

Chris raised an eyebrow. 'Before or after dinner?'

She saw the funny side of that and laughed. 'After, of course.'

He grinned. 'That's what I thought. For a girl who's as small as you, you eat like a horse.'

Tiffany lifted her chin and struck an elegant pose. 'But a very well-bred horse.'

'Oh, definitely,' Chris agreed, and put his arm across her shoulders as they came out of the lift.

It was some time later, when they'd finished their meal and were sitting over coffee, that Chris said, 'Why do you want some time off? Do you want to visit your family or something?'

'You know I haven't any family.'

'What happened to them?'

Picking up her cup, she drained it, then said, 'Are you ready to leave? I'll go and fix my face while you pay the bill.'

She went to stand up, but Chris reached across and put his hand over hers, stopping her. 'Why won't you tell me about your family, about your past?'

Leaning forward, anger in her eyes, Tiffany said curtly, 'Because it's none of your damn business.' And, wrenching her hand free, she got up and strode away.

A couple of days later they flew to Chicago, but the weather was bad and they had to detour round a storm so they were late getting in. They took a cab to the hotel where Chris had made a reservation and found that his client's representative was already there, waiting for him.

'You go up to the room,' Chris told her. 'I'll join you as soon as I can.'

Once there, Tiffany kicked off her shoes and un-packed her suitcase, then sat down by the phone and ordered coffee and sandwiches from Room Service, giving them the number of the suite. An hour or so later the phone rang.

'Is that Mr Brodey's room?' a female voice asked.

'Yes, that's right.'

'Oh, hello there. I'm Norma Beaumont. My husband is the company director you've flown down to meet with. I'd like to invite you both to have dinner with us tonight at our home. Would that be convenient for you?'

'Why, that's very kind of you, Mrs Beaumont. I'm sure we'd love to, so long as Chris hasn't made any other arrangements.'

'Well, I told Larry—that's my husband—to ask him so I'm sure it will be fine. Shall we say seven-thirty? I'll give you the address just in case Larry forgets.' She dictated it, then said, 'Until this evening, then. I'm so looking forward to meeting you, Mrs Brodey.'

'Oh, but Chris and I aren't——' But Mrs Beaumont had already rung off.

Tiffany gave a mental shrug and thought no more about it. But that evening, when they arrived at the Beaumonts' house and Chris went to introduce her, he only got as far as saying, 'This is Tiffany,' before Norma Beaumont came forward to shake hands and draw her into the sitting-room, saying, 'Oh, but I've already spoken to your wife on the phone. What a lovely name. Do come in, my dear. Is this your first visit to Chicago?' And the opportunity to put things straight had gone.

Chris was frowning, but Tiffany found the situation rather amusing, especially when, during dinner, Mrs Beaumont bemoaned the permissiveness of young people nowadays. 'The way some of them live together without getting married; I think it's just terrible. Don't you agree?'

'Oh, quite,' Chris answered, his face mask-like.

'How long have you been married?' she asked him.

Tiffany had to look down at her plate to hide her laughter, but Chris hardly turned a hair as he said, 'Not very long.'

'I didn't think so.' their hostess said delightedly. 'I could just tell that you were newly-weds—and so much in love.'

Tiffany stopped laughing abruptly and choked a little, and it was Chris's turn to throw a sardonic look at her.

After dinner, Mr Beaumont took Chris off to his den to see his collection of miniature drink bottles, while Mrs Beaumont, obviously a romantic, settled on the settee for a cosy chat, asking Tiffany all about her wedding. Taken aback at first, Tiffany soon entered into the spirit of it and described a magnificent ceremony in Oporto Cathedral, a wedding-dress with a train ten feet long, appointed Calum as best man, and with some relish cast Francesca as matron-of-honour.

'Really?' The older woman's eyes widened in exquisite delight. 'Chris's cousin is a real princess?'

'Only by marriage. And they are divorced now.'

'But even so—a princess,' she said in awe. The door opened as Chris and her husband came back, and Mrs Beaumont said animatedly, 'Your wife has just been telling me all about your wedding, Chris. It must have been magnificent, in a cathedral like that, and with a princess for a bridesmaid.'

Chris's eyebrow rose and he shot Tiffany a look that spoke volumes. 'Yes, it was—er—beyond imagination.'

They left shortly afterwards and Chris didn't say anything in the taxi, but when they reached the hotel he said shortly, 'So what was the idea of telling them we were married?'

'I didn't; Mrs Beaumont assumed it.'

'You didn't have to keep up the pretence by telling her a lot of lies about a fancy wedding.'

Tiffany dropped into a chair, smiling in remembrance. 'She asked, and I had to tell her something. She loved the bit about Francesca.'

'And you just loved making it up.' Coming across to her chair, Chris put a hand on each arm and loomed over her. 'And I notice you've been signing the hotel chits with my name.'

'You should have reserved the room in both our names instead of just your own, then. As you're so particular about who uses your damn name,' Tiffany said, her lip curling.

'Just don't get any ideas.'

For a minute she didn't understand, but then she pushed him violently away and stood up. 'I can't believe you said that! Do you really think I'd want to *marry* a louse like you? God, you're such an arrogant, conceited pig! I'd rather walk the streets than marry into your family!'

Chris's face tightened. 'Then what the hell are you doing here?'

'I'm not *married* to you.' Her chin came up and her eyes flashed defiance and pride. 'You're not *good* enough to marry me.'

He gave an angry laugh. 'Good enough! That's rich. Your one object in crashing our garden party back in Portugal was to try and hook Calum. If you could have caught him you'd have married Calum like a shot.'

'No, I wouldn't—because I'd have found out what rotten hypocrites you all are in time. He's as big a louse as you are,' Tiffany yelled in anger. And, taking off her shoes, she threw them at him.

Chris ducked, then came after her, his jaw thrust forward, menacing anger in his eyes. Seeing the danger, Tiffany turned to run for the bathroom, but he caught her and pushed her back against the wall. She flailed at him with clenched fists, but he caught them and held them above her head. 'So you're too good for me, are you?'

'Yes, I damn well am,' she said breathlessly, struggling to get free.

'But you're not too good to take what I give you. Because I'm rich—and that's why you're here. And that's why you'll do whatever I want. Won't you?' Forcing her wrists together, he held them in one hand, and with the other dragged up her skirt. 'Won't you?'

'No!' She struggled again and tried to knee him, but he laughed, his free hand busy. She felt the dominant hardness of his body and gasped, struggling again. But that only served to increase his forcefulness. Passion spread through her like an erupting volcano; she gave a low moan of acceptance and took the thrust of his virile manhood.

From then on, Tiffany always took great care not to be mistaken for his wife. They went back to New York, resumed their normal life, although shortly afterwards Chris left her behind for a week when he went to Madeira for the House of Brodey's bicentennial celebrations on the island.

Alone in New York, Tiffany expected to have a wonderful time and planned visits to museums and art galleries, cooking for herself for a change. She carried out her programme, looked at paintings and exhibits, but found that they didn't hold her interest as she'd expected. Even cooking was no fun when there was only her to eat it. She felt restless, unable to enjoy herself. Time and time again she found herself going to the window and looking out into the deep, cavernous shadow of the street, or up into the small patch of blue above the skyscrapers. It came to her quite suddenly that she was lonely. Unbelievably, she was actually missing Chris.

The realisation stunned her. Tiffany dropped into a chair and stared at the wall, trying to see into her own mind, analyse her own feelings. But there was no getting away from it; she had got used to living with him, to having him always around. It came to her that this was what marriage must be like: feeling incomplete when the other was away. But she and Chris weren't married; she was only his mistress; he'd made that plain enough. Not that she wanted it any other way, except for them to part completely, of course. But without her realising it he had become such an important factor in her life that she was fast losing her individual identity. It was just sex, she told herself. It was that she'd got used to and now missed, nothing else. But she was filled with a great fear and resolved in future to remind herself constantly just how much she hated Chris and his cousins.

To take her mind off Chris, Tiffany wrote a humorous piece about a foreigner's view of shopping in New York, using his computer to type it up. Her powers of observation were good and she had a dry wit that she was able to convey on paper without losing sympathy for her subject. The next step was to spend several hours doing careful research to find which journal to send the article to. Deciding to go for the best first, then work down, Tiffany sent the piece to a national glossy, at the same time buying several large envelopes as she was sure it would soon come winging back with a rejection slip, whereupon she would immediately send it off again to the next journal on her list.

The evening before he was due to return, Chris rang the apartment. Tiffany was there but, guessing it was him, she didn't take the call, letting the answering machine take the message instead. But she listened, and felt a conflict of emotions at the sound of his clipped voice. He didn't say much, just the time of arrival of his plane, then paused before adding, 'It would be nice to be met.'

But she didn't go to meet him, instead making a point of being out when he got back. It was late in the afternoon when Tiffany at last strolled into the apartment. Chris was sitting at his desk, working on the computer. He looked up when she walked in and was still for a moment, waiting for her to speak, but when she didn't he said brusquely, 'Where have you been?'

'To an art exhibition.' Going to the drinks cabinet, she poured herself a gin and tonic. 'It's hot today.' She sat down in an armchair, and only then said, 'Did you have a good trip?'

'Well, thank you for asking,' Chris said with heavy irony. 'I take it from the warmth of your welcome that you didn't exactly miss me.'

'That's right,' she lied calmly, 'I didn't.'

He frowned, looked as if he was going to say something biting, but then shrugged and turned back to his desk. He had the safe open, Tiffany noticed as she sipped her drink. She knew that her passport was in there, but didn't know the combination of the safe. Soon after their arrival in New York she had gone through his desk, looking for the number, but Chris kept it in his head. He was busy on the phone and using the fax machine, catching up on the urgent work that had accrued while he'd been away.

Tiffany finished her drink and went into the bedroom to shower and change. But instead of getting dressed immediately she went through to the kitchen in her bathrobe to fix herself another drink, feeling hot and thirsty again.

Chris was still using the phone. When he put the receiver down, he stretched his arms then moved his head as if his neck ached. 'Are you any good at massage?'

'I don't know; I never tried.'

'Well, come and try now.'

He got up and went into the bedroom, sat on the edge of the bed. Reluctantly she followed him, and saw that he looked very tired. He had already taken off his tie, and now he pulled off his shirt so that she could kneel behind him and knead the taut muscles of his shoulders and neck. She didn't know if she was doing any good, but he closed his eyes and didn't complain.

'Why are you so tired?' she asked. 'Is it jet-lag?'

'That and the time-difference, I suppose.'

'Were your parents OK?'

'Yes, fine.'

'I expect they were pleased to see you. You ought to go there more often.'

He grimaced wryly, then opened his eyes and said, 'Francesca and Calum were there. She's coming to New York soon.'

Tiffany's hands grew still. 'Why is she coming?'

'To do some shopping, I think.'

'For her wedding, I suppose.'

Chris stretched his neck. 'She isn't getting married that I know of.'

'I thought she was set to marry her French count?'

He shook his head. 'No, that's all off—if it was ever on. She's coming here just to shop and look up old friends.'

'Here? To this apartment?' Tiffany's voice rose. 'If she comes here I'm leaving! There's no way I'm going to live under the same roof as that skyscraper of a cousin of yours.'

Chris laughed at the description, turned and caught hold of her hand. 'You don't have to; she's going to stay with a friend.'

'I'm surprised she has any.'

'She went to college in America; she has a host of friends over here,' Chris said reprovingly. 'Just because you're jealous of her it doesn't mean that——'

'I'm *not* jealous of her,' Tiffany cut in. 'I just can't stand her, that's all. She's as arrogant as Calum—and you.'

Letting go of her hand, Chris said shortly, 'I thought you were supposed to be giving me a massage.'

'If you want a massage, then go to a massage parlour. I'm not a——'

But Chris gave an exclamation of annoyance, twisted round and pulled her down on to the bed. 'Anything I want you to be. Remember?' he said with something close to a snarl. Putting his hand under her chin, he looked down at her for a moment, his eyes angry, then he bent to kiss her.

Whenever he'd tried that before, she'd always jerked her head away, and he had got the message and given up trying, but now he forced her head back, laughed shortly, and took her mouth. Tiffany immediately bit his lip, hard. Chris gave an exclamation of pain and outrage, and suddenly they were fighting, rolling on the bed as Chris tried to dominate her and she resisted in every way that she could.

'You little bitch! I'll teach you to bite me,' Chris snarled.

He put a hand in her hair, but Tiffany raked his chest with her nails and squirmed out of his hold. She went to get off the bed but he caught her and pulled her down on top of him. Bunching her hand into a fist, she hit him on the chin and swore at him, but the blow hurt her hand more than him. Chris laughed and swung her under him but Tiffany brought up her knees and managed to push him off. Again she tried to get off the bed, but Chris grabbed hold of her sleeve. The already loosened robe came open and she slid out of it, but almost tripped as he suddenly let go. With an athletic bound, he caught her again, and put both arms round her in a bear-hug, pinioning her arms to her sides.

Tiffany swore at him and tried to struggle free. She was so hot, panting, beads of perspiration on her skin. Chris, too, was breathing hoarsely. He put a hand behind her head and moved his body against hers, the skin of his chest hot against her own. She felt his tiny male nipples against the budding firmness of her own, could feel the muscles in his arm holding her like a steel belt. Tilting her head back, she opened her mouth to give a gasping moan, and then her hands were at his belt, fumbling in their eagerness, urgent for him to take off the rest of his clothes.

He hardly had time to kick them off before Chris was carrying her back to the bed, taking her in a storm of hungry passion that carried them both to the heights of excitement. He cried out in prolonged pleasure, his jaw thrust forward, his body arched in spasm after spasm of sensuous delight.

Tiffany's own cries of rapture were drowned under his, and afterwards, when Chris lay by her side in total exhaustion, she knew that this had been the best time of all. Their fighting had been a kind of savage foreplay that had added intensity and fire to what both had known was the only possible outcome. Anger and defiance: his anger had been inevitable from the moment she had walked in the door and ignored him, just as his trying to kiss her had led inevitably to her defiance and their fighting. And both had led to the most wonderful sex she'd ever known.

Chris stirred, the hammering of his heart almost back to normal. Putting a possessive hand on her breast, he said complacently, 'Now tell me you didn't miss me.'

'Go to hell,' she responded, which made him laugh.

Gathering her into the curve of his arm, Chris almost immediately fell asleep. Tiffany lay still for a while, letting her own body recover, trying to store up the memory of how wonderful it had been, but knowing it was impossible to re-create such overwhelming sensations. It could only be repeated in reality. And only with the same man? Not for the first time Tiffany wondered if it was the enmity between them that engendered such fantastic sex. Did hatred light such a consuming fire?

She had never known love, couldn't really imagine what it could be like, despite everything she had read and heard. And she certainly couldn't imagine it lifting her to even greater pleasure than hatred had given her. If it could, then it must be wonderful beyond words. But life had made Tiffany a realist, and she didn't believe it would ever happen to her—not now. She grimaced to herself and thought, Well, even if my body has been used, at least my heart is still mine, still free. Then she laughed with inner irony; lord, what a stupid, sentimental load of rubbish.

She felt hot again. Sliding out of Chris's embrace, she got off the bed and glanced down at him. He was fast asleep. But then, he had looked very tired. On an impulse, she bent to pull the duvet over him, but then stopped herself. Let him pull up his own covers.

Going into the kitchen, she got a drink of water, turned to go back to the bedroom to shower and dress, then came to a sudden stop. The door of the safe was still open.

CHAPTER SIX

CAREFULLY setting down the glass, Tiffany went to the bedroom door and softly closed it. The next moment she was at the safe, searching through it for her passport. She found it quickly enough, but as she hastily pulled it from the pile of documents inside the safe several others fell out on to the floor. Cursing, she bent to pick them up, and was surprised to find an envelope marked 'Not to be shown to Francesca. Destroy at appropriate time'.

Intrigued, Tiffany hesitated for only a moment before putting some water in the kettle and setting it to boil. The envelope was an old one and the gum dissolved easily. What it contained was dynamite. Her mouth falling open, Tiffany hurriedly read the contents. It was an agreement signed by some man who was being paid a considerable sum to stay clear of Francesca, and was dated six years ago, when Francesca would have been at college. The agreement was signed by the man—and by Calum!

Afraid that Chris might wake, Tiffany hid the document in a drawer in the kitchen, between the pages of a booklet telling you how to work the washing machine, knowing that Chris would never find it there. She would read it through properly the next time she was alone. What, if anything, she was going to do with it Tiffany as yet had no idea. But just to have the knowledge gave her a great advantage over Francesca, and maybe over Calum and Chris.

Going to the bedroom door again, Tiffany opened it a crack to check that Chris was still asleep. Back at the safe, she had a closer look at its contents. There was a wad of money. With that and her passport she could go anywhere in the world and start a new life. But the temptation only crossed her mind for a moment; the passport was rightfully hers, but not Chris's money. There were a lot of business documents in the safe, the lease for the flat, which she saw belonged to the Brodey company rather than Chris, and a bundle of letters, most of them in female handwriting and addressed to Chris and Calum. From ex-girlfriends, she presumed, and strangely felt no desire to read the ones for Chris but a great curiosity to read those for his cousin.

Putting her eye to the crack in the door, she saw Chris stir and roll over. Tiffany hesitated, longing to read the letters. Would he notice if she took them out? If he found her passport gone he would; he'd inevitably check everything in the safe. She bit her lip, saw him move again. Instantly making up her mind, she took the letters addressed to Calum from the safe but put her passport back, then hid the letters away, picked up her glass of water and crept back into the bedroom and across to the bathroom. With a sigh of relief she closed the door and would have locked it if there had been a key, but Chris, objecting to being locked out, had removed it long ago. She drank down the water thirstily, then ran a bath.

A few minutes later she heard Chris moving about, then he came into the bathroom. Lying back in the bath, deep, with expensively scented foam, Tiffany closed her eyes and ignored him as he showered.

When he came out, he said, 'Want your back scrubbed?'

'No.'

He laughed. 'Maybe I'd better not at that. Otherwise I'll never get any work done.' But even so he swept aside some of the bubbles then bent to kiss her nipples as they peeped, rosy and tantalising, above the water. 'God, that's so damn sexy,' he murmured, straightening.

'You have bubbles on your nose,' she told him.

He grinned, wiped them off with his finger and plonked them on to her nose instead.

Tiffany didn't go into the sitting-room again until she'd dressed to go out for dinner. She knew he would have found the safe open, would have wondered if she'd been in there, so she carefully avoided looking in its direction as she crossed the sitting-room to the kitchen to get some ice for another drink. She knew that Chris watched her as she did so, but she merely said fretfully, 'I feel so hot.'

'Maybe you're coming down with a bug.'

Only then did she turn in his direction. The safe was closed now. 'I hope not.'

'Perhaps we ought to stay in this evening.'

'But I'm hungry. Aren't you?'

'Yes. But I noticed there's some stuff in the fridge. It looks as if you've been catering for yourself while I've been away.'

'I don't like going out to eat alone.'

He raised a quizzical eyebrow. 'And there was me thinking that you'd be out looking for a new meal ticket.'

Her tone sharpened at his unfairness. 'I don't want to be kept. I want to be like any normal woman and have a job, be independent.'

'Your job is to keep me happy.'

She gave him a disdainful look. 'Any woman could do that.'

Chris's mouth twisted wryly. 'No, not any woman.'

'But why me?'

He got to his feet and stood looking down at her. She looked particularly good tonight, fair hair like golden silk, her petite but perfect figure enclosed in a cream sheath-dress with a gold belt, her legs and delicious ankles shown off to their best advantage by her high-heeled shoes, and her blue eyes looking at him from under finely arched brows, with such puzzlement in their depths. He shook his head in wonder. 'You really don't know, do you?'

'So tell me.'

For a moment he seemed to hesitate, but then gave a short laugh. 'Because you hate me, of course. Because it amuses me to make you do what you keep telling yourself you don't want to do.'

She gave him a look of contempt. 'Well, that figures. I always thought it was because I ignored you when we first met, that I was more interested in Calum.' He shrugged and she said tauntingly, 'If he'd made me the offer you did, I'd have jumped at it immediately.'

'Tut-tut.' He shook his head at her. 'And who said just now she wanted to be independent?'

'Independent of *you*, yes. When are you going to let me go?'

'You know when. We agreed—when I tire of you.'

'And when will that be?' she demanded petulantly. Chris didn't answer, and her eyes suddenly widened. 'Why, when I stop hating you. That's it, isn't it? If I fawned all over you, got possessive and demanding, you'd get rid of me like a shot.'

Not answering the question directly, Chris said, 'Does that mean you're going to change your attitude towards me?'

'It's a temptation. A very great one. But somehow, even to gain my freedom from you, I don't think I could bring myself to be that hypocritical. It would be too nauseating.'

For a moment Chris's face grew grim, but then he shrugged and said sardonically, 'That's what I love about you—your sweet and charming manner.'

Tiffany gave a mocking smile in return. 'Well, that's good because I'm never going to change.'

'That's what I thought.' He stood up and pulled on his jacket. 'Let's go and eat.'

They went out to the nearest restaurant, a French bistro-type place where they were becoming known, but when they sat down and looked at the menu Tiffany found that her appetite had gone. She ordered just a small salad but left most of that. 'The air-conditioning in here must be fierce,' she said, shivering, putting her hands up to rub her bare arms.

'No, it's no cooler than usual. Are you sure you feel OK?'

'Yes, of course.'

But Tiffany refused coffee, which she usually liked to linger over, and made no objection when Chris suggested they go straight back to the apartment. There he put his hand on her forehead and said, 'You're burning up. I'd better call a doctor.'

'No, it's probably only a cold or something. I'll take some aspirins and I'll probably be fine in the morning.'

Chris tried to argue but she was insistent and snapped at him not to make a fuss, so he eventually said, 'All right, all right. We'll see how you are in the morning.'

Tiffany took the pills and got thankfully into bed, and was even more relieved when Chris got his stuff and said he'd sleep in the spare room.

'I'll leave the door open so call me if you need me.'

'I won't need you. Just go away and leave me alone.'

He gave her an exasperated look but did as she asked. Tiffany fell into a restless sleep, pushing the covers aside as she became unbearably hot, troubled by a dream about her mother that she'd had often in the past but not for some time now. She woke with a cry and put a hand up to her throat. Almost immediately Chris came into the room, belting his robe round him.

'What is it? Hey, you're soaking wet. You must be running a temperature.'

'No, it was just a bad dream. But I'd like a drink.'

He brought her a glass of water and she drank it down thirstily, her throat feeling tight and sore.

'Thanks. I'm OK now.'

She lay back on the pillows but he stayed beside her, gently stroking the damp hair back from her forehead, a frown between his eyes. 'What was the dream about?'

'I've forgotten,' she said, so quickly that he knew it was a lie.

'Won't you share it with me?'

'No. I don't want to share anything with you.'

'You live with me,' Chris pointed out.

She was silent for a moment, then said tiredly, 'But I'm not a part of you—and I never will be.'

She fell asleep again, but in the morning was so obviously unwell that Chris called the doctor without even asking her. The man came promptly, looked her over and told them that she'd caught a particularly nasty flu bug that was doing the rounds. 'Stay in bed for a week and don't take any other medication while you're taking the antibiotics I'm prescribing for you,' he ordered. Turning to Chris, he said, 'Will you be able to take care of your—er——?'

'Girlfriend,' Chris supplied. 'Yes, I can work from home.'

'No, I want a nurse,' Tiffany said with croaky determination.

The doctor looked amused. 'It seems the young lady doesn't trust your nursing capabilities.'

'I'll take care of her,' Chris repeated.

He did, too. He brought her an endless supply of drinks and made her swallow her medication. When her nightdress got soaked with sweat he helped her change into a dry one, and he had the maid come in every day to change the bedlinen and cook a meal. And during the whole time she was ill he slept in the spare room.

It was a long time since Tiffany had been looked after by anyone, and she had mixed feelings about it. She didn't like having to be grateful to Chris; she'd rather it had been anyone but him. She rather suspected that he enjoyed having her dependent on him, probably because she obviously hated it so. And she thought that it must give him some kind of erotic pleasure to bathe her hot body, to brush her hair, to sit with her as she lay helpless; why else would he do it?

It was over a week before she'd recovered enough for him to leave her alone in the flat, and almost a week more before he came back into her bed. When he did so he was surprisingly gentle, but this angered her; their relationship was built only on concupiscence, not tenderness. She didn't want to be held as if she might break, be stroked lightly, or have him kiss her neck and throat while he murmured soft words in Portuguese that she didn't understand. Those were the kind of things a husband would do, a lover, somebody who cared about you. But Chris was none of those things; he'd told her himself that their relationship was based on nothing more than cupidity aroused by his amusement at her open defiance and dislike of the situation in which she found herself. So she pushed his hand aside and said brusquely, 'Do you want me or not?'

He did of course, taking her now in anger instead of tenderness, but still satisfying them both.

The next day he went to the office early and Tiffany remembered the letters she'd hidden away. Taking them from their hiding place, she first looked again at the document that had bought off the man Francesca had been involved with. His name was Andy Sims. Had they been in love, the two of them? Obviously Francesca must have been, but the man...? Surely he wouldn't have allowed himself to be bought off if he'd really loved her? But he'd taken the Brodey pay-off, and quite a large sum at that. So maybe he had been out for what he could get. What had Francesca been told? Tiffany wondered. It was clear that she knew nothing about the agreement. Had the man told her that he'd tired of her? Had he just disappeared from her life? And had she been very upset at the sudden end to her love-affair, probably her first romance?

It was intriguing, not only because Tiffany had reason to hate Francesca, and because she was Chris's cousin, but because Francesca aroused interest in everyone she met. She was that type of girl, so vital, so beautiful, so—classy. A classy bitch. Yes, those were the words that best described her. This man who had been paid off had, in Tiffany's opinion, been lucky. It was impossible to imagine Francesca, with her love of expensive clothes and possessions, ever being happy with someone poor enough to be bribed. If she'd married him, she would have made this poor Andy Sims' life a hell on earth with her demands.

Thinking about Francesca made Tiffany remember that she'd been due to visit New York. Had she come and gone while she, Tiffany, had been ill? More than likely. If she had seen or called Chris, and learnt that Tiffany had the flu, that would certainly have kept her away. Not that they would have met anyway. Neither girl would have wanted it, and Chris would definitely have wanted to make sure that he didn't get caught in the middle.

Picking up the other letters, those addressed to Calum, that she'd borrowed from the safe, Tiffany saw that she'd been right: the letters were from a woman. These too were old, dated many years ago. It was difficult at first to make sense of them, because they referred to other people by name—people whom Tiffany didn't know—but they were definitely love-letters. The woman who wrote to Calum poured out her heart to him, regretting they couldn't be together, longing for the day when they could meet. But they would have to wait until Simon went away. Whoever Simon was. But it didn't take long for Tiffany to realise that Simon must be the woman's husband. So Calum had had an affair with a married woman. The naughty boy!

Tiffany had picked the letters out at random, and there were gaps, but the envelope with the latest date turned out to contain a letter ending the affair. Tiffany read it, then sat up, goggle-eyed. From what the woman said, it was clear that she was expecting Calum's child but had decided to pass it off as her husband's. Wow! This was the kind of stuff the gossip columnists must dream about! The Brodeys were certainly turning out to have several skeletons tucked away in their wall safe. And yet Calum had dared to take such a high moral tone with her.

It would just teach them a lesson, she thought, if this information was used to expose them for what they really were—as human and subject to temptation as anyone else. What a great article it would make for the magazine back in Portugal that had asked her to do a piece on the family, or for any one of the more salacious gossip magazines, Tiffany thought with a laugh of amusement. She could almost name her price and the Brodeys would never live it down. It naturally occurred to her that she could write the article herself, but the thought crossed her mind only fleetingly; even though theirs was a business arrangement, she still felt some loyalty to Chris and had no intention of embarrassing him or upsetting him. So far he had kept his side of the bargain: she had a wardrobe full of clothes and he took her out to places where she could wear them. She wanted for nothing—except the freedom to leave. And a settled future—she lacked that too. She had been on the move from one place to another most of her life, and had an unspoken longing to have somewhere of her own.

She hid the letters away again, realising that she would have to figure out some way of getting them back into the safe without Chris knowing. But there was no rush; they had been locked away in the family safe for years now and it was hardly likely that anyone would go looking for them after so long.

The next day the telephone rang while Chris was in the shower, so Tiffany answered it. It was Francesca. There was a short silence when Francesca heard her voice, then she said, 'I want to talk to Chris.'

'Well, hello, Francesca,' Tiffany said mockingly, adding pointedly, 'I'm fine, thank you so much for asking. And how are you?'

'I couldn't care less how you are,' Francesca retorted. 'Get Chris.'

'Ask nicely and I might,' Tiffany teased.

'Is he there or isn't he?'

'Oh, yes, he's here.'

'Then stop playing around and just get him.'

'Did it ever occur to you to say please?' Tiffany demanded, her voice hardening.

'Not to you, I don't,' the other girl returned. 'Haven't you got enough out of Chris yet? Why don't you leave him alone? You're ruining his life.'

'*I'm* ruining his life?' Tiffany gave a laugh of disbelief. 'How *dare* you say that to me?'

'I dare because it's true. He's obsessed with you. You're just a cheap little——'

'Don't call me names, Francesca,' Tiffany broke in with warning menace in her voice. 'Just don't do it.'

'I shall call you whatever I damn well please. Women of your type shouldn't expect anything else.'

Angry now, Tiffany said tauntingly, 'What's the matter, Francesca, having man trouble—trouble in finding one that you can walk all over now that Michel has ditched you?'

There was a gasp on the line. 'I have *not* been ditched. It was the other way round. Michel was very sweet, but I——' She broke off. 'Why don't you mind your own business? Just get Chris.'

'I will when you say please.'

'You disgusting little tramp!' Francesca shouted, and slammed down the phone.

She called again half an hour later and this time Chris took the call. 'Hello, Francesca.' His glance flicked to Tiffany and she knew that Francesca must be talking about her. Chris frowned and said, 'Yes, of course I'll meet you to say goodbye. Where and when?' He made a note in his diary, then put down the phone. 'It seems you and Francesca had another row,' he remarked.

Tiffany gave a small laugh. 'She seems to have a chip on her shoulder about something. Was she in love with her husband when she married him?' she asked curiously.

'Why do you ask?'

'Is she regretting splitting with him?'

Chris went over to the drinks cabinet and made a couple of Martinis. 'I shouldn't think so. It was perfectly obvious after the first year or so that it wasn't going to last. She tried to make it work, tried hard, but she should never have married him.'

'Why did she?'

He handed her a glass. 'Why does anyone get married? Because she thought she was in love with him, of course.'

'Could she have been on the rebound? Had she ever been in love before?' Tiffany asked casually, but watching closely for his reaction.

Chris shrugged. 'How should I know? I expect she had infatuations, the same as everybody else.'

An ambiguous answer that didn't tell Tiffany whether he knew about Francesca's former lover or not. Probably not, she thought, because she was beginning to be able to read his reactions by now. Although there were still times when his features became a mask and she couldn't understand him at all.

Sitting down next to her on the sofa, Chris put an arm along the back and said, 'Why so interested?'

It was her turn to shrug. 'She just seemed to fly off the handle very easily, that's all.' Tilting her head, she gave him an assessing look, wondering what secrets about him the safe contained. 'Have you been infatuated, then?'

'Of course. Loads of times. Haven't you?'

But she said, 'And have you ever been in love? Really in love?'

He looked down at his glass, twisted it between his fingers and didn't answer.

'Well?' Tiffany insisted, beginning to get curious.

He looked up, gave one of his rueful grins. 'I thought I was once, but she married someone else.'

'Really? Who did she marry?'

'My cousin.'

Tiffany stared. 'Calum?'

'No, of course not. Lennox.'

'Oh, you mean your cousin who lives in Madeira. The one who's married to Stella, the girl who's pregnant,' she said, remembering Stella's radiant happiness in her marriage and forthcoming child.

'That's the one. Only I ended up bringing them together. And she isn't pregnant any longer. She had her baby a couple of weeks ago.'

Tiffany was instantly diverted. 'Oh, you didn't tell me. What did she have?'

'A boy of course.'

She laughed. 'Why of course?'

'Stella always gets her priorities right.'

Tiffany laughed again at that, her face lighting up as it always did when she was amused and happy. But it was something she seldom did when they were alone together like this. Chris let his hand drop a little and touched her hair lightly. 'How about you—have you ever been in love?'

A closed look immediately came over her face. 'No, of course not.'

'There's no "of course" about it. Why haven't you? Haven't you ever met anyone?'

Moving away from his hand, she leant back against the sofa. 'Falling in love is a mistake.'

'That sounds as if you speak from experience.'

'Yes, I do.'

'But you just said that you've never been in love,' he pointed out.

'Perhaps it would be more accurate to say I speak from observation. I've seen what it can do to—to people.'

'To anyone in particular?'

But he was getting too close, and she got lightly to her feet. 'I feel like seeing a film tonight. How about you?'

But for once he wasn't to be put off, and said, 'Why won't you ever tell me anything about yourself? We've been living together for nearly three months and I know very little more about you than I did on the day we met.'

'I didn't know you had to submit a c.v. for this kind of job,' Tiffany returned tartly.

'It isn't a job, it's a relationship.'

She was walking through to the bedroom to get her bag, but stopped in the doorway and turned to look at him. Francesca's voice, telling her that Chris was obsessed with her, came into her mind but was immediately dismissed. Chris was merely piqued because she hadn't fallen for him. He expected her to change, but when he finally became convinced that she wouldn't then he would let her go. And she would still retain some pride. So her chin came up and there was cool defiance in her eyes as she said, 'Not to me it isn't.'

Chris got to his feet, came over and put his hand on the door-jamb. 'Not at the moment, perhaps. But when we're in bed together, when we make love, then it becomes a relationship—because you can't help yourself. You like it too much.'

'You're wrong. It isn't making love, it's just having sex. And to me it will never be anything more than a job—a job I can't wait to leave.'

Chris's mouth thinned and he put a hand on her arm. She felt it tighten and thought that her denial might have turned him on, that it was what his libido fed on. She waited, feeling the tension in him, expecting him to pull her into the bedroom, to undress her or order her to take off her clothes. For a moment it looked as if he was

going to, but then he turned abruptly away and said, 'If
you want to take in a film, then let's go.'

'I'll get my bag.' But Tiffany didn't move straight
away, instead looking at his broad back in puzzlement,
and with a feeling that was bordering on disappointment.

During the next couple of days, Tiffany felt strangely
low and unsettled. When Chris was out she looked again
at the document that had bought Francesca's boyfriend
off. Was she being unfair to them? she wondered. After
all, Francesca had been very young, and the boy too,
probably, and he would have had immense pressure
brought to bear on him to give Francesca up. The money
might just have been to move him geographically away
from her, to put him through a different college or
something. In her imagination, Tiffany had this Andy
Sims pining for Francesca still, and perhaps the break-
up of the latter's marriage had been because she was still
in love with him.

There was an address in Connecticut on the document.
Impulsively Tiffany looked up the number and called it.
A woman answered, but her voice sounded middle-aged.

'Is that Mrs Sims?'

'Yes, it is.'

'I'm trying to trace Andy Sims. Does he still live
there?'

'No, he doesn't. Who's calling?'

'I'm a friend of his from college,' Tiffany improvised.
'I'm in the States from Europe and I thought I'd look
him up.'

'Well, he lives in California now. I can give you his
number if you like.'

'Please.' Tiffany copied the number down, feeling that
her guess had been right. 'Er—could you tell me, is Andy
married yet?'

There was amusement in the woman's voice. 'No, he's still single, and no mention of any marriage plans.'

Tiffany thanked her and put down the phone with a sentimental smile on her face, thinking how nice it would be if Andy and Francesca could get back together.

People should be allowed to lead their own lives, make their own mistakes, but Tiffany was tempted to take a hand in Francesca's. She had reason enough to hate the other girl but had to admit to herself that at first she had liked her. And, if she was being honest, then maybe Francesca did have some excuse for her prejudice and dislike, too. But maybe, if Tiffany told her about Andy Sims, the two might get back together and Francesca would be grateful to her, a friend instead of an enemy. It would be nice to have a friend, even if she was a Brodey.

A call to Chris's secretary at the office elicited Francesca's telephone number and the time and place of his appointment with her. Then Tiffany rang Francesca and left a message with her friend, asking her to meet Chris half an hour earlier.

Francesca was already at the restaurant where she had arranged to meet Chris when Tiffany arrived. When Francesca saw her, her eyes widened in amazement. Then she said in sharp concern, 'Has anything happened to Chris?'

'No, he's fine. I wanted to talk to you before he came.'

'I suppose it was you who altered the time, then?' Francesca bent to pick up her bag. 'Of all the nerve! Well, I certainly don't want to talk to you.'

'You should stay,' Tiffany warned. 'I want to help you.'

'Help me!' She laughed in disbelief.

'Yes. You see, I—learnt something that may be of great importance to you. I really think you ought to stay and listen.'

Francesca eyed her narrowly, but put her bag down again. 'Is this something to do with Chris?'

'No, with you.' Tiffany paused, wondering how to go about this. It had seemed an easy thing to do when she'd had the idea, but when actually facing Francesca, with antagonism in every line of her face, it was somewhat harder. 'Look, your marriage—did you go into it on the rebound?'

'*What*?' Antagonism turned to outrage.

'Were you in love with someone else, someone you— lost?'

Francesca stared at her, and for a moment Tiffany thought she saw a flash of remembered pain in the other girl's eyes. But then Francesca said angrily, 'What the hell are you talking about? And just what right do you think you have to ask me such personal questions anyway?'

'I know it sounds intrusive, but I do have a reason. As I said, I want to help you.'

'I do not *need help*.' The words came out too quickly, with too much emphasis, almost as if she was afraid. Seeming to realise it, Francesca snapped out, 'And I especially wouldn't need it from a tramp like you.' With an impatient gesture she waved away a waiter who had come up to the table. Her face pale, she went on, 'How dare you presume on your—your dirty little liaison with Chris to meddle in my life? You may have gatecrashed our party and gatecrashed Chris's life, but I'm not going to let you do it to mine.' Leaning forward, she said, 'I can't wait for the day when he gets over this obsession with you and sees you for what you are.'

'Obsession? You said that before. But all it——'

'Of course he's obsessed with you,' Francesca cut in. 'He was supposed to stay in Madeira for another couple of weeks, but he cut the visit short to get back to you. And it's even affecting his work: when I got to New York his office said that he hadn't been in for over a week. And he wouldn't come and see me, just made some lame excuse about you being unwell. And he's cancelled several business trips he was supposed to make during the last month.'

'It was true; I was ill.'

'I don't believe it. Chris can't stand illness. He'd run a mile rather than be with someone who's sick. It was you who deliberately kept him away from me—out of spite.'

Tiffany was getting really annoyed; she had come here for Francesca's sake and all she was getting was a load of abuse she didn't deserve. But she made one last try. 'It's about Andrew Sims.'

Francesca immediately looked down, hiding the panic, the vulnerability in her eyes. When she raised her head a moment later her face was a complete blank, but Tiffany couldn't see her hands convulsively tightened into fists under the table. 'Who?' She shrugged off the name, but her voice was unsteady as she said, 'Don't try and change the subject. Just get away from Chris. And get out of our lives!'

She hadn't even remembered him! So much for first love, Tiffany thought disgustedly. Francesca was just as self-centred and uncaring as she'd supposed. Angrily she stood up, knowing that she'd wasted her time. 'Nothing would give me more pleasure. You and your precious family are all the same—arrogant, conceited, heartless parasites! And for your information I can't *wait* to get away from Chris—because I hate him as much as I hate the rest of the Brodeys!'

Her voice had risen and everyone within earshot was watching them. Tiffany swung away from Francesca's look of stunned surprise, went to stride away, and stopped short as she saw Chris standing just behind her. His face was white, a frozen mask of rage, and the glance he threw her chilled her to the bone.

'Get out of here,' he snapped at her, then walked across to where Francesca was getting to her feet.

Tiffany hesitated a moment, in no mood to be ordered around, but realising that Chris was in no mood to listen to her side of it either. And, come to think of it, there was no way she could tell him why she'd come. With an angry shrug, she left the restaurant.

As she strode along the street, still furious, it came to Tiffany that now Chris would have to let her go; he wouldn't want to keep her with him after this. She would be free. Free to make a new life for herself somewhere. But, strangely, this brought no great elation; she would rather they had parted in boredom than anger. Lifting a hand, she hailed a cab and went back to the apartment, pulled out her luggage and started packing her clothes. All she had here was clothes; she had no other personal possessions. Books and souvenirs, records and ornaments would have made it into a home, not a place where she reluctantly had to stay, and she definitely hadn't wanted that. So it didn't take long to pack. Now all she needed was her passport and the thousand pounds that Chris had promised her when they parted.

She'd expected Chris to follow her from the restaurant almost immediately, but he must have stayed with Francesca because he didn't come. Tiffany strode angrily up and down for a while, waiting for him. So much for sentimentality. So much for trying to help someone, she thought with resentment. She certainly wouldn't try that again. Francesca could just go ahead and ruin her life in the way she'd already started. Still feeling bitter, she sat down at Chris's computer, switched it on and, still furious, began to write a vitriolic exposé of the Brodeys and their sordid affairs. She named names, quoted dates and figures, left nothing out.

Writing it was therapeutic; much of Tiffany's anger had gone by the time she'd finished and polished the article. Reading it through, she laughed to herself, thinking what a furore it would create in the exalted circles in which the Brodeys moved. If it was ever printed. Which it wouldn't be. She had saved the piece as she'd worked, but now went to delete it; however, the sound of Chris's key turning in the lock pulled her up short and she quickly switched off the machine.

She was standing in the middle of the room, prepared to take his fury, her cases at her feet, when he walked in.

He saw the cases first, then looked up at her expectant face. He was still seethingly angry; she could sense it beneath the surface, see it in the cold steel of his eyes and the tautness of his features. 'Where the hell do you think you're going?' he demanded with something close to a snarl.

'You'll want to be rid of me now so I'm ready to go.'

'Is that why you did this—to make me so angry I'd kick you out?'

'Does it matter, if that's what it has achieved?'

Striding forward, he gripped her arm. 'Yes, it damn well matters. Why did you do it?'

She wasn't about to tell him the truth, ashamed now even of the sentiment that had prompted her to talk to Francesca, so remained silent. Which, of course, made him even angrier.

He shook her, his jaw thrust forward, his mouth a thin, menacing line. 'You think you're clever, don't you, rowing with Francesca in a public place, shouting my name out for everyone to hear?'

Tiffany found that she wasn't immune to his anger. She hadn't wanted it to be like this, hadn't wanted to upset him. Trying to end it, to get away from emotions of her own that she didn't understand, she said more curtly than she'd intended, 'Just give me my money and I'll go.'

He made a sound of disgust. 'Money! That's all you're interested in. That's the only reason you're here.'

'You promised me a thousand pounds when we split up,' Tiffany insisted, not bothering to contradict him.

He laughed unpleasantly, his anger still close to the surface. 'But we're not splitting up. Because I haven't finished with you yet. If you think you can coerce me into letting you go this easily, then you're very much mistaken.'

Her mouth dropped open a little as she stared at him. 'You mean—you want me to stay?'

'Yes.' His grip tightened as his eyes glinted down at her. 'For this!' And, picking her up, he swung her over his shoulder and carried her into the bedroom.

Afterwards, when he'd gone back to the office and she was lying alone, staring up at the ceiling, Tiffany remembered Chris's accusation that she cared about nothing but money. It was true that he gave her money for her everyday needs and paid for her clothes, but she'd rarely asked him for any extra, and she had enough clothes now to fill her wardrobe so hadn't bought anything much for some time. And he'd never bought her the kind of presents mistresses were supposed to get: jewellery, a sports car, that kind of thing. He was far from mean, but he'd had no right to say that. How would he like it if he were in her position? she thought indignantly. Entirely dependent on someone else, having to go to bed with them whenever they wanted.

Only she'd wanted it too. Tiffany's thoughts went back to the sexual act she'd just experienced, which had started in anger but ended in overwhelming pleasure, for both of them. Was it his anger with her that had turned him on again? Was that how he got his kicks? But she knew it wasn't so, because Chris had made love to her many times without being angry, and it had been just as good. Well, almost as good; she had to admit there was a certain added excitement when his passion was aroused so wildly. Sighing, Tiffany turned on to her side. One thing was for sure: when Chris still got this much pleasure out of it, he wasn't going to let her go whatever she did.

He came home that night looking moody, but he didn't mention Francesca again. Tiffany was afraid that she might have remembered who Andrew Sims was, and asked Chris how she, Tiffany, came to know the name, in which case he would guess that she'd looked in the safe. She waited nervously for him to ask, but gave a sigh of relief when he suggested they send out for a pizza and have it in front of the television set because there was a football match he wanted to watch.

So life went on as before, until two days later, when Tiffany went down to collect the mail and found a letter addressed to her, not Chris. She'd had a couple of letters from Isabel in Oporto, but apart from that she'd never had any mail before. Almost at once she saw that it was from the magazine she'd sent her humorous article to. Tearing open the envelope, her excitement running high, she read that the article had been accepted. And enclosed was a cheque for five hundred dollars!

Tiffany spent the whole morning deciding what she would do with the money. Her first thought was to buy a ticket to England, but she still hadn't got her passport.

She could, however, go somewhere in America, perhaps on a train or a bus. She let her imagination run wild, but soon came back to reality; five hundred dollars wouldn't last very long and then where would she be? Maybe she could buy herself something. But she had plenty of clothes and her life had been uncluttered by possessions for so long now that she couldn't think of anything to buy. A present for someone else, then? But there was only Chris, and she could just imagine his re-action if she gave him a gift. So what, then? What could she buy? The answer crept into her mind, filled it, and wouldn't go away.

Heading for the nearest bank, Tiffany changed the cheque into dollar bills. When Chris came home that evening he found a trail of them leading to the bedroom and the bed, on which the rest of the bills were spread. Tiffany was sitting in a chair by the bed, fully dressed, arms folded.

'What's all this?' he demanded with astonishment.

'It's your pay.'

'My *what*?'

'You heard me. It's your pay—for your sexual ser-vices. So don't just stand there; take your clothes off.'

CHAPTER SEVEN

CHRIS stared at her. 'Did I hear you right?'

'Is there something wrong with your hearing?'

'You know there isn't.'

'Then you heard me right. But just to make it absolutely clear...I'm paying you to do what *I* want—and I want to sit here and watch you strip.'

'What kind of game is this, Tiffany?'

'You think it's a game? Perhaps it is. A turn-on game. The type of game you like to play with me as the toy. Only now it's my turn to play it—and you're the toy-boy,' she added coldly.

Leaning against the door-jamb, Chris folded his arms, his eyes intrigued, but an amused, mocking curl to his mouth. 'And what if I don't want to play your games?'

'You don't have any choice.' Her face hardened. 'If you don't do what I want, then you won't get paid, you won't be fed or clothed, you'll get kicked out. Are you getting the picture?'

His brows drew into a frown and an emotion she couldn't fathom showed momentarily in his eyes, but then, his voice growing curt, he said, 'Where did you get the money?'

'Oh, you don't have to worry, it isn't yours. It's mine. I earned it.'

'Earned it? How?' he asked on a suspicious note.

'Not how you think,' she answered with contempt. 'I wrote an article for a magazine. I got paid five hundred dollars for it. And this is how I've decided to spend it.'

'You wrote a magazine article?' he said in surprise. 'What about?'

'That needn't concern you. All that matters is that I have the money to pay for your services. And five hundred dollars is really rather generous. So why don't you get started? Or do you want some soft lights and music to put you in the mood? *You* don't usually bother with all that, of course, but I'm willing to make a concession as this is your first time—the first time you've been used.'

Chris's jaw hardened and a bleak look came into his eyes. His voice rough, he said, 'Do you really hate me that much?'

'Yes,' Tiffany answered without hesitation, her chin rising.

For a moment longer he stared at her, then he swung round to go out of the room.

'Coward!' she yelled after him.

He stopped, turned to face her.

'Come back and find out what it's like! Come back and find out why I hate you.'

Slowly, Chris walked back into the room, his gaze fixed on her tense face, on her eyes that seemed to burn into his. Tiffany sat back in her chair. 'Now do it!' she said forcefully.

It was a full minute before he moved, then, almost as if it was against his will, Chris's hands went up and he began to undo his tie.

When the idea for this had come into Tiffany's mind she had seen it as a way of getting back at Chris, of punishing him even. Perhaps for being a man, and rich, and arrogant. For him thinking that he owned her. She'd wanted him to know how it felt to be used. And she'd intended just to sit there and watch, devoid of any feeling, so that he would experience for himself what it was like to be just a sex object.

But somehow it wasn't working out the way she'd planned. She'd had to bury feelings close to guilt when she'd taunted him for being a coward—inborn emotions that she knew an emancipated woman ought not to have. Men were no longer the master race, ruling women by their strength and the protection that strength gave them. All that was past and she had as much right to do this as he had—to humiliate him. Only there was no humiliation in his bearing as Chris slowly took off his clothes. Instead there was irony in his eyes, in the set of his jaw. And he watched her all the time, as if it were her who was on show, not him.

She had seen his naked body many times before and hadn't expected to feel anything when she saw it now. But this slow uncovering of his tanned skin, of muscles and broad chest, of legs and thighs, created an ache deep within her that she hadn't bargained for. Her mouth felt dry, her chest tight. He just slowly took off his clothes, didn't pose or flex his muscles or act in any way like a male stripper, and yet she felt like a voyeur. But she couldn't look away. Neither could she meet the eyes that watched her so sardonically. He revealed himself completely to her, arrantly male and not at all ashamed of his nakedness.

Tiffany's tongue crept between her lips, moistening a mouth that was completely dry. 'Now get on the bed,' she ordered hoarsely.

'On the money?'

Now at last, her eyes came up to meet his. 'Yes. On a bed of money. That's where I want you, where you belong.'

His jaw hardened and she thought that he was going to disobey her, almost wanted him to, but then he crossed the room and lay on the bed. She fumbled at her clothes, pulling them off anyhow, but Chris was looking up at the ceiling, ignoring her.

She knelt beside him on the bed and reached out to explore him, as he had so often explored her, her hands stroking the softness of his skin, caressing him intimately. He didn't touch her, just lay back and let her do it, but his eyes were on her face all the time. Tiffany had carefully planned what she was going to do next; she was going to arouse him, get him really aroused, then tell him to go to hell—because she didn't want him after all. The first part of the plan was more than successful: as she caressed him Chris's hands tightened into fists. He shuddered with awareness, gasped, then gave another gasp that turned into a low moan.

'You want me, don't you?' she said softly, her hands still busy.

He had closed his eyes but now he opened them and looked at her. But he didn't answer. Not that it mattered; his body spoke for him, spoke volumes!

Gathering up an armful of dollars, Tiffany scattered them over him. 'Well, you'll just have to make do with this—because I don't want you!' And with a laugh of triumph she turned to swing herself off the bed.

Chris surged upwards in one movement and grabbed her round the waist. 'Oh, yes, you damn well do!' he said forcefully, pulling her down beside him.

And she did. She did. Even though she resisted him at first, so that they rolled among the crumpled money, soon she was crying out in throbbing excitement, clinging to him as she arched towards him, her body ever eager for the pleasure he could give, knowing that this was what she had subconsciously hoped for all along.

Usually, after they'd had sex, Chris would hold her in his arms while their pounding hearts quietened, until she rolled away from him to let him know that she didn't want to be close. But tonight he didn't attempt to hold her, just got up and went into the bathroom to shower. Tiffany slowly sat up, looked round rather dazedly at the dollar bills all over the bed and the floor. What was she supposed to do with them now? she wondered. Somehow it had gone sour, her clever idea. It was she who had been humiliated, not Chris. Yet again she had been betrayed by her own body.

Tiffany sat with her head in her hands for several minutes, then put on her robe and, with a set face, began to pick up the money. She hated it now, wished she'd never had such a crazy idea. When she'd picked up all the bills, she put them in a bag and stood staring at it; she almost felt like crying. The wail of an ambulance out in the street filled the air, a sound so familiar now that she didn't usually take any notice. Tonight, though, it reminded her that there were thousands of people far worse off, that her problems were as nothing in comparison. Her frown clearing, Tiffany put the bag aside, to be given tomorrow to a place where it might do some good.

Chris came back into the bedroom, glanced at the bed, but made no comment. He began to take fresh clothes from a drawer. 'Hurry up and get dressed,' he said curtly. 'I want to go out and eat.'

She took a few steps towards him, and lifted a hand as if to put it on his shoulder, an apology hovering on her lips. But Chris's back was turned implacably towards her, and after a few moments Tiffany lowered her hand, then went into the bathroom to obey him.

Their relationship, or whatever you cared to call it, altered from that day onwards. They still slept together and Chris still took her often, and they went out for meals as before, sometimes with Chris's friends. He even took her with him on a couple of business trips, where she didn't do him any harm at all when it came to getting orders, her natural charm winning over the clients as much as Chris's sales pitch. But he had changed towards her, his manner becoming more withdrawn, losing a lot of his humour and openness. It was almost as if he was on guard all the time, watching his own words and actions.

So what? was Tiffany's first reaction. I couldn't care less. Maybe now he'll let me go. But it was impossible just to disregard his manner, impossible not to be affected by it. A tenseness grew between them, so that it was a relief when Chris went to the office. And yet Tiffany found herself waiting for him to come home, and looking eagerly to see if he had changed, hoping that he was his old self again. They'd used to talk together quite a lot, about things that were in the news, even argue heatedly sometimes when their viewpoints didn't agree. Now, though, they didn't talk much at all, Chris often turning on the television set as soon as he returned in the evening.

Tiffany felt snubbed and knew it was her own fault. Knew, also, that she ought to be glad, but somehow wasn't. She didn't like this tense atmosphere, this feeling of enmity between them. Only in bed were they close, and it was still good, but even there it wasn't quite the same. Chris never attempted to kiss her now, and always turned away afterwards, lying on his side with his back towards her, not holding her a moment longer than was necessary, not murmuring words in Portuguese. In the mornings he got up and left her in bed, instead of making her get up and have breakfast with him as he'd used to. She didn't care, of course, but somehow she didn't sleep very well at nights, which made her feel headachy and unwell the next day.

A week or so later, in the middle of the morning after Chris had gone to work, Calum turned up at the apartment. Chris hadn't mentioned that he was coming to New York, but he had spent longer at the office the last couple of days and had gone out alone one evening. Calum didn't telephone first, just turned up on the doorstep. When Tiffany opened the door and saw him, she stared in astonishment. Instinctively she knew that his coming could only be bad news, so she went to slam the door, but he simply put his shoulder in the way and walked straight in.

With a sigh, she said, 'Hello, Calum,' adding sarcastically, 'Do come in, won't you?'

His eyes swept round the flat before he turned to look at her, his mouth set into a grim line. 'Well, at least you haven't redone the place in feminine fripperies.'

'Haven't emasculated it, you mean,' she returned coldly. 'Chris isn't here, if you're looking for him.'

'I'm not. I know where he is.' He sat down on the sofa. 'It's you I came to see.'

She ought to have guessed that he'd turn up eventually, Tiffany supposed, sitting opposite him. Francesca must have gone running to him, and he would have guessed that she'd looked in the safe. Had he told Chris? she wondered on a sharp pulse of anxiety, and then couldn't understand why it mattered. Biting her lip, she said, 'What do you want?'

Calum's eyebrows rose a little, and he gave her a searching look. 'Are you unwell?' he asked reluctantly.

She looked at him in surprise, unaware of the dark circles around her eyes and the paleness of her cheeks that showed because she wasn't wearing make-up this early in the day. 'No, I'm fine,' she told him, adding, 'Thank you,' in some puzzlement because she hadn't expected him to ask or care.

Calum frowned, but said brusquely, 'You can guess why I'm here. We had all hoped that by now Chris would have—would no longer be interested in you.'

Tiffany gave a short laugh. 'You mean you hoped he would have got tired of me and kicked me out; isn't that what you're trying to say?'

His eyes came up to clash with hers and she met them squarely. 'Yes, I suppose I am. We—his family—are concerned about him. We want him to live a normal life.'

'"A normal life"?'

'It's time he was settling down. Looking round for a wife.'

She laughed again. 'Chris had the reputation of being a womaniser; I take it you'd rather he do that—play the field—than be with me. Is that it?'

'You're no good for him, Tiffany. If you care about him at all——'

'I don't,' she cut in, so curtly that Calum's face tightened in contempt.

'So you're in it just for the money!'

'What else? Come to that, what else is your family good for?' she added insultingly.

His eyes blazed, but Calum kept his temper. 'I'm willing to pay you fifty thousand dollars to leave him—and stay away from him,' he said curtly.

His words seemed to hit her like a blow in the stomach, made her feel physically sick. Her face and jaw grew tense as she fought down the nausea. She had thought that words could never matter any more, but they did; they mattered terribly. How dared this arrogant fool sit there and insult her like this? How could he despise her so much that he could even think that she would accept his offer? But he did despise her; they all did. To them she was like Andy Sims, all those years ago—a nuisance

to be bought off. Sitting back in her chair, the sem-
blance of a smile on her face, she said over-brightly, 'No,
thanks. I don't think so.'

Calum gave her a weary look. 'I'm not here to haggle,
Tiffany.'

It would have been interesting to know how much he
would have been willing to go up to, but she said, 'Nor
am I.'

He gave her a glare. 'What do you want?'

'From you? Nothing.'

After hesitating only briefly, Calum said, 'All right,
I'll make it sixty thousand.' Opening his briefcase, he
took out a typed document. Tiffany smiled inwardly,
knowing exactly what it would say. 'In return you will
have to sign this undertaking that you won't bother Chris
again.'

He held the paper out to her but she didn't even bother
to look at it. 'I don't think so.'

Calum's face hardened. 'If you think you can get Chris
to marry you, then I can tell you now that you won't
succeed. He may be besotted with you at the moment
but he has enough sense to know that it won't last, and
that no way would you be welcome in our family. So
you would be much better advised to take the money
I'm offering you.'

He was lying through his teeth, of course. Tiffany
knew that there was no way he would have made her
this offer unless he was afraid that Chris would commit
himself to her irrevocably. Although why he should think
so she had no idea. Chris had certainly never mentioned
marriage, and she had made it plain enough that to stay
with him a moment longer than she had to was the last
thing she wanted. But that had been between the two of
them, of course; to outsiders, seeing the possessive way
Chris treated her, their relationship might seem com-

pletely different. It was ironical, really; here was she longing to leave and Calum was offering her the money to do it. He would probably also know the combination of the safe and could get her passport out of it. There was everything here she needed to get away from Chris and the Brodeys forever.

Getting to her feet, she shook her head. 'I'm not going to take your money—and I'm not going to leave.' She added the last deliberately to goad him, to punish him for thinking that she could be bought.

'If you think you can push up the price, you're mistaken. That was my last offer.'

'I've already said no.'

Still he stayed where he was. 'I can make things extremely uncomfortable for you, Tiffany. You would be wise to take the money.'

'No, thanks.' She looked down at him, wondering why she had thought him so devastating when she'd first met him. OK, he certainly had classical good looks, but his whole character seemed to lack warmth. She could never imagine him being obsessed with any woman, let alone being passionate in bed, whereas Chris—— Her thoughts broke off abruptly. Why on earth was she thinking along these lines when neither cousin was of any interest to her? 'And please don't threaten me. Any harm you do to me you will only do to Chris—and I'm sure you don't want that.'

'Now who's doing the threatening? You may well regret this, Tiffany. Remember that Chris could tire of you and throw you out at any moment.'

She shrugged. 'Perhaps.'

'Then why take that chance? Why not take the money I'm offering and go now?'

Seeking for some way to annoy him, she said, 'Maybe he will marry me.'

Contempt showed in every line of his face. 'You'd marry someone you don't love, just for money?'

Suddenly angry herself, Tiffany said fiercely, 'I'm tired of living from day to day. I want to have a future. Do you know what the biggest luxury in my life would be? To have something to look forward to. To know that I'll be in the same place in five years' time, even in ten years' time. To know that——' She broke off, her hands clenching, and gave a short laugh. 'Not that you'd ever understand, of course—you Brodeys in your ivory towers.'

For a long moment Calum gazed up at her, then he got slowly to his feet. 'You're a strange girl, Tiffany. I could almost wish...' But then he shrugged as his face hardened again. 'Here's my card. You can reach me or leave a message for me on this number. When you decide to take up my offer, call me. But you'd better make up your mind soon because it won't be open indefinitely.'

She didn't attempt to take it so he reached out and put it in the pocket of her blouse, brushing her breast. Her eyes blazed with fury, startling him. 'Get out, Calum. Just get out.'

It took a while for her to simmer down after he'd gone. She strode up and down the room, thinking how little she deserved this, how much she hated the Brodeys. Thinking about it, she was overcome by nausea again and had to rush to the bathroom to be ill. She came out, still shaking, and made herself a cup of strong coffee, feeling miserable. Only then did it occur to her that she had a hold over Calum that she could have used to turn the tables on him, to threaten him in return. But the next second she knew she wouldn't have done so; she wasn't yet so desperate that she needed to throw the Brodeys' dirt in their faces. It also intrigued her that Calum hadn't brought up her confrontation with Francesca or questioned her about her knowledge of Andrew Sims. She could only think that Francesca hadn't told him, for reasons of her own—or because she had forgotten her teenage sweetheart altogether; that was far more likely, Tiffany thought cynically.

When Chris came home he still said nothing about Calum being in New York. She could have told him that Calum had been to the flat, about his offer, and perhaps have stirred up some trouble between the cousins, but Tiffany didn't. She felt tired, drained, and strangely lonely. She could almost wish that Chris would talk to her again as he'd used to; even sparring with him would have been better than this reserve that was building up between them. At this rate Calum would hardly have needed to bribe her at all. It couldn't be much longer before Chris threw her out. But he was a very virile man; perhaps he was waiting to find someone else before he got rid of her.

Tiffany didn't sleep very well again that night, and crept out of bed to go and sit on the sofa in the other room. She didn't switch on the lights, but sat in the darkness, lost in her own thoughts, wondering rather drearily what she would do when Chris finally tired of her.

The door to the bedroom opened suddenly, making her jump. Chris flicked on the lights and strode into the room, stopped when he saw her. His shoulders drooped, as if they'd been tense, but his voice was harsh as he said, 'What are you doing out here?'

'I couldn't sleep. I didn't want to disturb you.'

He came over to her. He was wearing only a pair of silk sleeping-shorts, his upper half bare. 'Come back to bed.'

Why she didn't know, but Tiffany held out her arms for him to pick her up. He did so and she put her arms around his neck, her head against his shoulder. She felt him stiffen, and let her lips trail down his throat. It had been a couple of days since they'd had sex; he would want her now. Chris carried her to the bed and laid her on it, then went back to turn off the lights. When he returned, he stood looking down at her for a moment. Again, she held out her arms to him.

Chris stared, frowned, said, 'Tiffany?' on a hoarse note. She didn't answer, just looked up at him, lips parted, her eyes enormous. He gave a strange sigh, and the next moment was beside her and had taken her in his arms.

She was still asleep when he left the next morning, but when she woke Tiffany had to rush to the bathroom and was ill again. Only later, when she looked at the breakfast she'd prepared and felt sick all over again, did it occur to her to get out her diary and work out some dates. Then she stared down at it, appalled; her periods weren't consistent—but she hadn't had one for two whole months!

But that was impossible; she was on the Pill. Maybe she had forgotten to note one down. Tiffany thought back, trying to remember, growing more anxious by the minute. Then it came to her; when she'd been ill the doctor had told her to take no other medication while she was on antibiotics so she'd stopped taking the Pill for a couple of weeks. She'd started them again immediately afterwards, of course, but perhaps there had been a few days when they hadn't been effective. It must have been then. Sitting at the breakfast-bar, Tiffany stared into space, her heart and mind filled with dismay.

Her first thought was to blame herself for being such a fool. She should have realised, should have known. The doctor should have warned her. But there was no point in allotting blame; it had happened and that was it. Now she must decide what to do. The first thing, she supposed, was to make absolutely sure that she was pregnant. OK, then what? But Tiffany shied away from even thinking about that. All she knew was that Chris would be absolutely furious with her—and convinced that she had done it on purpose to try to trap him into marriage. It came to her that her life was a mess, always had been and always would be. She was just like her mother—no good to herself or anyone else.

At the thought of her mother Tiffany's hands tightened and she had to bite her lip hard. Resolutely she pushed the memories aside, dressed, and went out to try and find a place where she could have a discreet pregnancy test.

A couple of hours later Tiffany was sitting in a park feeling close to hysterical laughter. She had the addresses of several places where she could go, but found that she didn't have enough money for the test. And she had given away a whole five hundred dollars only days ago! Now she would have to wait until Chris gave her some more spending money. Although that might be some while if he thought she still had the fee for her article. The only other way she could get any cash quickly was by selling some of her clothes, which she was reluctant to do: she had bought expensive things of good, classical design that were destined to last for several years, until long after Chris had tired of her. Things that she could wear to work once she got a job.

Or at least that had been the idea; now everything had changed. When Tiffany got to her feet, there was only one thing she was sure of: no matter what the result of the test, no matter how ill she felt, she must conceal this from Chris. No way did she want him to accuse her of setting out to trap him. She could imagine his voice, almost hear the words he would hurl at her—he and his cousins. Tiffany smiled grimly; Calum would think she'd done it deliberately to push up the price.

She had intended to ask Chris for some cash that evening, but when she got back to the apartment she found a message from him on the answering machine saying that he wouldn't be home till late. Was he having dinner with Calum, or with another woman? She ought to hope it was the latter, that he would soon get rid of her for someone else. Then she could take her money and get out of his life before he found out what had happened. But somehow the thought of Chris with another girl—taking her out, putting a possessive hand on her shoulder, making love to her in their bed——
Their bed? Since when had it been that? It was Chris's bed, nothing to do with her. But the mental pictures aroused new and angry emotions within her, emotions so unfamiliar that it took her a couple of days to realise they were born of jealousy.

She pretended to be asleep when he got home late that evening, and by staying in bed the next morning until after he had left for the office she was able to hide the bout of morning sickness from him. The day seemed a very long one, but when Chris came home she was devastated to find him much warmer towards her than he had been recently. He came in, kissed her on the cheek and told her she looked gorgeous. She hadn't expected this, had expected him still to be withdrawn and cool, and it took a few minutes to realise that it must have been the night before last, when she had welcomed him into her arms, that had changed him.

Tiffany didn't know whether to be pleased or sorry. To her that night seemed light-years away, and she didn't feel that she could cope with his new behaviour. But, anxious to hide her worries, she somehow managed to pretend to be very animated and witty when they went

out to their favourite restaurant to eat, putting on an act
as she had so often done before. It pleased Chris; he
laughed a lot and was happy. So maybe there wasn't
some other girl. The profound feeling of relief that swept
over her made Tiffany realise at last that she'd felt
jealous. But that was, of course, ridiculous. She hated
Chris, so how could she possibly feel jealous about him?

It was a question she had to put aside because Chris
was talking and she had to concentrate on what he was
saying. He liked her to be attentive, and as he was telling
her about a business trip to Mexico he was planning—
for both of them—it was more than easy to listen and
exclaim with apparent pleasure. They sat over their coffee
for a while, but it was too hot to go dancing or to a
club, and they went straight from the restaurant to the
apartment.

When they got there Tiffany, not wanting to ask him
directly for money, said casually, 'I've run out of cab
fares.'

Chris looked amused and merely said, 'I suppose you
spent the money you got for your article?'

'Yes.'

'You never told me what the article was about.'

'Oh, nothing that would interest you—just feminine
stuff.'

'Where's the magazine?'

'It hasn't come out yet. I was paid on acceptance, not
on publication.'

Taking out his wallet, he fished out a hundred-dollar
bill. 'Is this enough.'

'Yes, thanks.'

He was sitting on the sofa, watching motor-racing,
but he held out his hand to her, and when she put hers
into it he pulled her down beside him. Then he put his
arm around her and held her comfortably against him.

It was a very small gesture, one that he had probably made lots of times in the past, when she would have reacted stiffly, unwillingly doing what he wanted. But lately, since that time with the dollar bills, he hadn't been at all friendly towards her, and his holding her close now made her realise just how much she had missed it. Her eyes were on the screen but she was blind to the cars racing round the track, was only aware of the strength of the arm with which he held her, the cool tang of his aftershave, the solidness of the body against her own. When he finally threw her out, she would never be with him like this again, never be held in the safety and strength of his arms again.

At the thought, a feeling of utter desolation filled her, an emotion so intense that she wanted to cry out against it. She wanted to throw her arms round him and beg him to hold her, hold her and never ever let her go! Closing her eyes tightly, Tiffany had to dig her nails into her palms to stop herself from doing it, to keep herself still beside him. After a long, long moment she slowly opened her eyes and relaxed her hands. Now she knew why she had felt so lonely these last weeks, why she had been jealous. Somewhere along the line she had made the fatal mistake of falling in love with the man who had bought her, the man she hated.

When the race ended, Chris flicked off the set, turned and kissed her neck. 'Let's go to bed,' he said, his voice heavy with need.

But Tiffany shook her head and lied to him. 'It isn't a convenient time.'

He groaned, but accepted it, and when they got into bed he contented himself with caressing her breasts, and soon afterwards fell asleep. But Tiffany lay awake a long time, silent tears coursing down her cheeks, knowing that she was in such an emotional state that if they'd made love tonight she would have told him everything. About being pregnant, about loving him, even about her past, everything.

The next morning she phoned the nearest clinic and made an appointment for the following day. When she kept it they told her it would take five days for the result of the test. Normally it would only take three days but that was Thursday and no one worked over the weekend.

Luckily Chris went to the office the next day, and the following morning he'd arranged a game of squash with a friend. Usually she went with him to watch, but that day she refused, saying, truthfully, that she felt unwell. Thinking it was because she had her period, Chris happily went off alone. For a while Tiffany stayed in bed, fighting the nausea, telling herself it was all in the mind. She got up to dress, but then had to rush into the bathroom and hang over the loo.

When she flushed it and turned around, Chris was there. He was staring at her, a stunned look in his eyes, and it was perfectly obvious that he had guessed the truth. But he did what she had done—went to her bag and emptied the contents on the bed, grabbed up her diary and flicked it open to run his eyes over the pages. Tiffany cleaned out her mouth, then took a shower before going into the bedroom to pull on some clothes.

Chris was waiting for her in the sitting-room, pacing up and down, his face like thunder. 'How long have you known?' he demanded curtly.

She didn't try to lie or to pretend; there was no point. 'I don't. Not officially.'

His head came up at that. 'You haven't had a test?'

'Yes, but I haven't had the result yet.'

'When will you get it?'

'Tuesday. They said to come back Tuesday,' Tiffany answered, pushing back a lock of hair.

'I thought you were on the Pill!'

'I am—I was—but I had to stop taking it while I was ill.'

He opened his mouth, and she just knew he was going to accuse her of lying, of having done this deliberately. She braced herself to take it, but he suddenly swung away and took an address book from the drawer of his desk, flicked it open and made a call. Evidently it was to his doctor. He spoke to him, asked him where he could get a pregnancy test done immediately. 'Yes, today,' he said. 'And I want the result today.' He noted down the number he was given, dialled it, spoke, made the arrangements he wanted, then said, 'Thanks. We'll be right over.'

Dropping the receiver, he caught her hand and hurried her outside to whistle up a yellow cab. When they were in it, she said dully, 'I thought you were playing squash.'

'My opponent rang the club to say he couldn't make it, so I let someone else have the court.' Chris gave a grim smile. 'I thought I'd hurry back so that we could go out somewhere for the day, spend it together.' He laughed. 'But I sure as hell didn't think we'd be spending it like this!'

She had nothing to say to that, even staying silent while she had the test done. When she came out Chris was reading a notice on the wall that said that the clinic did terminations seven days a week. The receptionist said, 'We'll phone you as soon as we have the result. It will take about an hour.'

Chris seemed about to say that they'd wait, but then walked ahead of her out into the street. He sat forward in his seat in the taxi on the way back, clasping and unclasping his hands, his face grim and remote. Tiffany found she couldn't bear to watch him, and sat gazing unseeingly out of the window. It was a lovely day, hot and sunny, but with enough breeze to make it really pleasant. Children enjoying the weekend with their parents were out in the park being pushed on swings or playing baseball. Family cars loaded with leisure stuff were heading out of the city.

When they got back to the flat, Chris made them both a drink, pouring himself a double gin and tonic. He gave a glass to Tiffany but he had forgotten to put any gin in it. Then he began to pace up and down again while she sat silently in a chair. The burr of the phone, when it finally came, sounded stridently loud. Tiffany jumped, although she'd been expecting it, and Chris strode over to pick up the receiver.

He said, 'Yes,' a few times, then replaced it. Slowly he turned towards her.

Her eyes wide and tense in her pale face, Tiffany waited for him to speak. When he didn't she said impatiently, 'Well? What did they say?'

His voice sounding strange, Chris said, 'The result was positive. You're definitely pregnant.'

She got to her feet feeling as if this wasn't really happening to her, that in a moment she would wake up from this bad dream. Still he didn't speak, and she had to force herself to say in an unsteady voice, 'So—so now what happens?'

Chris's eyes met hers, cold and bleak. Harshly he said, 'There's only one thing that can be done—isn't there?'

She stared at him, knowing he meant an abortion. 'Yes,' she answered curtly, fighting the pain in her heart. 'There is.' Then she walked past him and out of the flat.

CHAPTER EIGHT

IT WAS many hours before Tiffany returned to the apartment. She had been sitting on a bench in Central Park, oblivious to the people around her, seeing again the anger in Chris's face, knowing he thought she'd got pregnant on purpose to trap him. She hadn't, of course, but there was no way he would ever believe her. And now he expected her to destroy their child.

It never even crossed Tiffany's mind to do so. Now that she knew for sure she was pregnant she allowed herself for the first time to think of the tiny miracle inside her as a person, think of it with wonder and joy. It would be entirely her own, dependent on her, *needing* her. She put a hand on her stomach, willing the child to feel her love for it, letting it know that it was safe. But she must never let Chris know that she intended to keep the baby.

A wave of fear filled her as Tiffany thought he might somehow force her to have an abortion, make her life unbearable until she agreed. She must avoid that at all costs. And the cost would, of course, be to leave him. To go away and never see him again. Her eyes closed with pain at the thought; to leave Chris now that she'd fallen in love with him would be very hard. A laugh of bitter irony broke from her. Lord, how things had changed! All those weeks when she'd longed to be free of him, and now... And now she knew that she would miss him unbearably. But she had her child to consider. Tiffany's brow creased in a worried frown as she tried to think of a way to leave Chris without telling him that she was keeping the baby. In the end the answer was very simple; she waited for a few hours longer then went back to the apartment.

The way she looked gave credence to the lie she was about to tell. Her face, devoid of make-up, was very pale although there was an almost feverish look in her eyes. Usually these were of a deep, vital blue, but now there was a dead, washed-out look about them, and the smoky shadows around them were darker than before. Tendrils of damp hair clung to her forehead and her lower lip trembled until she became aware of it and closed her mouth tight to hide it.

Chris was waiting for her. The minute she walked in he said savagely, 'Where the hell have you been?'

Walking into the kitchen, Tiffany poured herself a glass of chilled mineral water and drank it gratefully down, her throat working.

Chris seized her arm the second she'd put the glass down. 'I asked just where you've been all day.'

Slowly she turned to face him. 'I've been—rectifying the situation.'

He stared at her. 'What's that supposed to mean?'

Lifting a hand, Tiffany pushed the hair off her forehead. She didn't answer directly but said, 'I'm through with you, Chris. I'm leaving.' She tried to pull away from him but he pushed her back against the cupboard.

'You're not going anywhere until I say so. Now tell me what you meant, where you've been.'

She looked at him with a face drained of all emotion, and said in a small, hard voice, 'I should have thought that was obvious. I've done what you wanted me to do.'

'What I wanted you to do?' Dropping his hand, Chris stared at her, his face tense. His voice cracked, unsteady, he said, 'What have you done?'

'You said there was only one thing to be done so I did it. I went back to the clinic and had an abortion.'

Tiffany let bitterness show through for a moment as she added acidly, 'They'll be sending you the bill.'

Chris's face went rigid with shock, then he cried out, 'No!' in a voice she didn't recognise as his, said it on such a note of anguish that she couldn't believe her ears. Then anger flooded through his face, filled his eyes. Clenching his hand, he brought it up as if to strike her and she instinctively flinched away, staring at him in utter disbelief. His fist an inch from her face, Chris stopped himself, but his whole arm shook as he fought to control his rage. His face twisted as the veneer of civilisation strove against the primitive urge to express his fury. Then he suddenly swung away from her and strode across the sitting-room into the bedroom.

Tiffany stayed where she was, a stunned look in her eyes, realising that she had got it wrong, that he hadn't wanted her to get rid of the baby after all. It took several minutes for the implications of this to sink in, and only then did she become aware of noises coming from the bedroom. Slowly she followed him there.

Her suitcases were open on the bed and Chris was throwing her clothes into them, tearing them from the wardrobe, hangers and all, and just tossing them at the cases. An armful of shoes was dropped on top of a silk suit; the gown she'd worn for the Brodeys' ball in Oporto was rolled up anyhow and thrown on top. Going to her drawers, Chris pulled them right out of the cabinet and just upturned them over another case. Then he went into the bathroom and came back with her stuff out of the cabinet, perfume and toothpaste landing on her delicate silk underwear, underwear he had once delighted in taking off her.

Tiffany just stood in the doorway watching helplessly until he had slammed the cases shut and clicked the fasteners. Picking up the cases, he carried then through into the main room, almost knocking her out of the way when she put out a hand to try and stop him. He dropped the cases by the door, strode to the phone and ordered a cab, then went to the safe, clicked it open and took out her passport and a wad of money. Thrusting them at her, his face still dark with fury, he snarled, 'Now get out! Get out of here.'

Tiffany put her arms behind her back, not taking them, and said, 'Chris, please listen to me. I——'

But he stuffed them down her blouse, the stiff passport scratching her breast, then, losing control, he grabbed her shoulders and shook her. 'You cruel little bitch! How could you do it? To deliberately make yourself pregnant and then, when you thought you could get nothing out of me, to just walk out and rid yourself of it.' She tried to speak but he shook her again, said furiously, 'You should have waited. Should have heard me out. Because there was no way I would have let you destroy it. But you didn't think like that, did you? You used it to try to trap me and when you thought it hadn't worked you——'

'Please, Chris, no! I didn't——' She shouted above his voice, but he wouldn't let her finish.

'All right, maybe you didn't do it deliberately, but you would still have used it, because to you it was just part of the game. Can't you realise that this was a *child* you destroyed? Our child? Didn't it mean anything to you?' Suddenly he laughed, and it was the most terrible sound she'd ever heard. 'But of course it didn't. Because you don't care about anyone except yourself. You wouldn't know how to love a child, how to love another human being, you cold-hearted little bitch. Calum and Francesca were right about you: all you want is money.'

'That isn't true. I——'

The entry-phone bell rang sharply. Chris swung away to answer it, said tersely, 'She'll be right down.' He picked up her handbag and thrust it into her hands, then opened the door.

'Chris, will you please listen to me?' she said desperately. But he had already picked up her cases and started down the stairs two at a time, too impatient to wait for the lift.

Tiffany ran after him but the passport fell out of her blouse and she had to stoop to pick it up, stumbling as she did so. By the time she caught him up, Chris was already outside and putting her cases in the cab. Grabbing his arm, she said forcefully, 'Chris, you have *got* to listen to me. You'll be sorry if you don't.'

But he rounded on her and said savagely, 'The only thing I'm sorry for is falling for you in the first place! Yes, that's right,' he said as she stared at him in shocked silence. 'I really fell for you, but you didn't even notice. And if you'd kept the baby I would even have married you.' He laughed in utter bitterness. 'You could have had it all, Tiffany, as much money as even you could want. Think about that when you're back in the gutter!' And, grabbing her arms, he pushed her into the taxi and slammed the door. 'Take her to the airport, Cabby, just as fast as you can go.'

'Hey, lady.'

Some minutes later Tiffany's stunned eyes blinked and refocused as she realised the cabby was talking to her. 'Yes?'

'If I was you I wouldn't go around with that wad of bills sticking out of your brassière.'

'What?' She glanced down. 'Oh, yes, of course.' She took the money out and put it in her bag along with her passport.

'Sounds like that was some humdinger of a fight you two had back there. He your husband?'

'No.' She blinked again and looked around. 'Where
are we going?'

'He said to take you to the airport. That where you
want to go?'

Tiffany thought, and reached the conclusion that she
had messed up her life yet again, really messed it up this
time. Dully she said, 'It sounds as good a place as any.'

The cabby laughed and tried to get her to tell him
what had happened, but when she just shook her head
he left her alone.

At the airport Tiffany pushed her trolley along, auto-
matically looking for the first flight to England. Chris
would never listen to her now, would never believe her
even if he did. So there was no point in staying; she
might just as well go home. No, that wasn't right: home
was where the heart was, and she had left her heart back
there with Chris. So it didn't really matter where she
went. She walked along, reading the boards, then stood
still. There was a flight leaving in two hours, not to
London but to Lisbon. Well, why not? she thought. Why
cold, rainy London when I can have the warmth of
Portugal? And it's much cheaper to live there than in
England. Maybe I could get a flat in Oporto. Maybe—
her breath caught—maybe I might even see Chris there.

It was the day of the *barco rabelo* race. The whole popu-
lation of the town of Oporto was massed on the banks
of the River Douro to watch. The boats were gathering
at the harbour bar, with their white sails, each inscribed
with the name of one of the port houses, for the moment
lowered. All the boats carried several wooden wine
barrels, the same barrels that they had once carried all
the way down the river from the *quintas* in the Alto
Douro region, running with the current, riding the white-
water rapids that had now been replaced by dams and
prosaic locks. A motor-boat carried the members of the

Confraria do Vinho do Porto from the quay, where the race was to finish, downriver to the start, the officials, resplendent in their robes and medieval-style hats, looking out of place on the modern boat.

They ought to have been riding in a Venetian barge from a Canaletto painting, Tiffany thought fancifully as she watched from the bank. A Klaxon sounded for the start, fireworks whizzed into the air as the *barcos* frantically raised their sails.

The flat-bottomed boats with their white sails caught the wind and raced towards the town, each striving to lead—and to avoid hitting the others. People began to cheer as soon as they heard the Klaxon, those near the finish shouting as much as the rest.

'Can you see them yet?' Tiffany asked Isabel, who was leaning out over the river wall.

'No, not yet.' Isabel leaned even further out, and Tiffany grabbed her, afraid that she would fall. 'Yes, yes!' The Portuguese girl squealed with excitement. 'I can see a sail.'

'Who is it? Is it Brodey's?' Tiffany peered round her, trying to see, as excited as everyone else.

'No, it is Sandeman. But now there are two more. I cannot see... One is Croft...' She swung round excitedly. 'Yes, the other is Brodey.'

'Where? Let me see.' Tiffany squeezed forward. 'Oh, yes! Come on! Come on,' she yelled in encouragement.

All the boats were in sight now and were bearing down to where they stood on the quay above the finishing line. Behind the leaders two boats bumped into each other and had to be pushed aside with boat hooks, the helmsmen at the great stern oars that steered the boats yelling curses. The leaders were closing on each other, but then the Sandeman boat tried to cut across the river to take advantage of the current, but got caught in the wash from a motor-boat. The Brodey *barco*, by a neat

display of helmsmanship, slipped through the gap this
created and took the lead.

The boat was in full sight now and Tiffany craned her
neck to watch and cheer it on, her blonde hair a beacon
of gold among the dark-haired Portuguese pressing
around her. Now she could see the sailors in their uni-
forms of red trousers, white shirts and gaily coloured
neckerchiefs, could even see their faces. And the first
one she recognised was Calum's. He was standing in the
prow, yelling instructions back to the helmsman who was
still hidden from her by the sail. Tiffany stopped shouting
to stare; she'd had no idea that Calum would actually
take part in the race; if anything she'd thought he would
be in some palatial house over on the other bank,
watching with his guests.

Her eyes scanned the other faces on the boat and she
recognised Calum's cousin, Lennox, and—surely that
was Sam Gallagher? What on earth was he, an American,
doing in a *barcos rabelos* race in Oporto?

The boat came nearer, fighting off the pursuing Croft
and Sandeman vessels, close to winning. Tiffany could
see the helmsman now as he crouched down to see under
the sail. It was Chris!

'Brodey! Brodey!' Isabel shrieked in excitement.

Almost home, Chris must have heard her and glanced
towards them. Tiffany, pressed into her place by the
throng, was unable to duck or hide. Their eyes met, and
even over that distance she could see the way his face
tightened. Bent over the great oar, he began to straighten,
forgetting what he was doing—and the boat crashed
smack into the quay!

There was a gasp of horror from the onlookers, then
Tiffany gave another gasp of her own, because Chris,
after shouting something to Calum, had swung himself
off the boat on to a ladder fixed to the wall of the quay,

was climbing it then pushing his way through the crowd towards her.

Tiffany's feelings were a mixture of hope and dismay. Had Chris missed her so much that he was overjoyed to find her again? Or was he still angry with her and furious to see her on his home territory? The latter, probably, knowing her luck. Either way, Tiffany didn't want to have to face him again among this crowd of people. Turning to Isabel, she said, 'Let's get out of here—fast.'

Reacting immediately to the plea in her eyes, Isabel began to cleave a way through the crowd for them, telling people that her friend felt faint. They good-naturedly moved out of the way, re-forming behind them. But the two girls had hardly broken through the worst of the crowd and begun to hurry up the hill to the town before Chris caught them up. Putting his hand on Tiffany's shoulder, he swung her round to face him.

For a moment his eyes seemed to devour her and her hopes rose, but then they hardened and he said curtly, 'I want a word with you.'

He began to march her back towards the quay, but Isabel bravely got between them and said, 'You leave her alone, you. You've caused enough trouble for Tiffany already.'

'Not half as much as I'm going to make,' Chris said, looking at Tiffany with menace in his eyes. His glance switched to Isabel who was standing determinedly in the way. 'Who are you?'

'This is my friend——' Tiffany began, but Isabel interrupted before she could be introduced.

'Yes, her friend. The one she was staying with when you got her kicked out of the boarding house where we live so that she had no place to go. And I will not let you hurt her again. If you try to take her away I will shout and scream.' And she stood, arms akimbo, glaring belligerently at Chris.

He gazed at her in astonishment, but didn't let go of Tiffany. 'Look, I don't know what you're talking about but I intend to talk to—to this woman, and there's no way you're going to stop me.'

Too angry to think in English, Isabel began to berate him loudly in Portuguese, but Tiffany put a hand on her arm, stopping her. 'It's all right, Isabel; he won't hurt me,' she said reassuringly, although, looking at Chris's face, she wasn't at all certain of that herself.

'I will not let you go with 'im,' Isabel declared, and turned to argue again, but just then a car pulled up beside them and Calum quickly got out.

'So you've found her. Good. Get her in the car.'

Looking at their faces, Tiffany drew back, puzzled and suddenly afraid. Surely just being here in Oporto was no reason for the anger that blazed from both cousins' eyes? It had to be more than that, but for the life of her she couldn't think what. Well, there was only one way to find out, and as they both looked as if they were quite capable of using force if she refused to go with them she said with dignity, 'If you wish to talk to me you only have to ask.'

'Get in the car, then,' Calum said curtly.

'Where are you going?'

'Somewhere where we can talk in private.'

Tiffany looked from one to the other of the men with great misgivings. There was such deep anger and hostility in both faces that some of her courage deserted her. 'I want Isabel to come with me. Otherwise you'll have to talk to me right here and now.'

Calum looked as if he was going to argue, but Chris said, 'All right. Let's go,' and he held the back door of the car open for them.

But when all four of them were in the car and driving away it seemed that they hadn't made up their minds because Chris said, 'We can't take them to the wine lodge—everyone will be going there to celebrate the race. It will have to be the house.'

'No,' Calum said. 'It's too far. The guest apartment in town is nearest. We'll go there.'

Chris didn't look too happy with it, but raised no objection.

The streets were almost empty but soon people would come flooding back from the riverside to fill the cafés and bars, to celebrate until dark, when they would go back to the river for the magnificent firework display that would end the day. But there was no one to see them as they pulled up outside the apartment building Tiffany remembered so well, and went up to the flat where Chris had first taken her to stay, and where they had made love for the first time. Her mouth twisted as she remembered; she had thought of it just as sex, but she ought to have known that it could never have been that good without love, even if she hadn't realised it then. Even if neither of them had.

His hand on her arm, as if still afraid that she might run away, Chris walked her into the flat, the others following. Calum went straight to the phone but Tiffany didn't hear what he said. Her thoughts were too full of memories. Her eyes went to Chris and surprised a pinched look about his mouth, a bleakness in his eyes. When he realised that she was watching him his face became mask-like, with no trace of emotion. She had seen the same thing happen many times before, and had always thought that he was shutting her out; only now did it occur to her that maybe he had been hiding his true feelings for her, afraid of jeering rejection if he had let her see how he really felt.

'Francesca will be here shortly,' Calum said, putting down the phone.

So it seemed that all the Brodeys were to condemn her. Shaking herself free of Chris's hand, Tiffany went and looked unseeingly out of the window. Isabel came to her side, giving her an uneasy look. Somehow Tiffany managed a smile for her. 'Go and sit down. I'm fine. Really.'

But Isabel stayed with her until Francesca entered the flat. Tiffany turned to face her, expecting to meet more fire and brimstone, but this was a different Francesca. There was a glow about her, a smile in her eyes, as if she was very happy. Moreover, she was wearing a simple skirt and blouse, open-toed sandals, and *not* a single piece of jewellery. If it hadn't been for her height, looks and inherent elegance she could have been any girl in the crowd. As it was, she made the simple clothes look as if they were designer originals.

Francesca looked at Tiffany, flushed slightly, and went to stand quietly by the other window!

Tiffany could hardly believe it; this was certainly a different girl from the one who'd had her thrown out of the Brodey *palácio* all those months ago.

Calum said, 'What we have to discuss is a very private matter. A family matter. I must ask your friend to wait in another room.'

Isabel began to protest, but Tiffany said, 'It's all right. I'll be fine. Please do as he asks. I'll call you if I need you.'

The Portuguese girl was still reluctant, but Tiffany persuaded her and eventually she went with Calum, who escorted her to the bedroom, shut the door, and locked it, pocketing the key.

Tiffany gave him a sardonic look. Crossing to an upright chair, she sat down on it. Keeping her eyes on Calum, she said, 'Well? What do you want, the three of you?'

Calum glanced at Chris for a moment, but then said cuttingly, 'While you were staying in New York you made it your business to pry into our lives. You managed to get into the safe and found out things that you were never supposed to know. There are—documents missing from the safe. We want to know whom you have sold those papers to.'

So it was that. Tiffany wished now that she'd never been tempted to look in the safe; if Chris hadn't locked away her passport she wouldn't have. With a small sigh, she said, 'You don't have to worry; I haven't sold your sordid little secrets.'

Chris immediately strode forward and pushed Calum out of the way to loom over her. 'Don't lie. I found the article you wrote about us on the computer.' He caught hold of her wrist. 'Who did you sell it to? What gossip-mongering journal bought it from you? Tell us!'

'I already have. I never sold the article.'

His hand tightening on her wrist, Chris said, 'For once in your life tell the truth. I *know* you sold the article—and you know very well why.'

She looked at him them, remembering the time they'd made love on the bed of money, when she had tried to humiliate him but had felt only ashamed of herself. Her eyes clouded, and she wondered if that had been the time he'd made her pregnant. God, that would be really ironical, she thought, her mouth twisting into a bitter smile.

'It isn't funny!' Calum said harshly. 'My God, I regret the day you ever came into our lives!'

Francesca had come forward; the three of them stood towering over her, all looking at her with condemnation in their eyes. Suddenly, gloriously, Tiffany was angry. Springing to her feet, she glared at them. 'No one,' she said fiercely, 'wishes that as much as I do! I've had it up to here with you Brodeys. Yes, I sold an article, but it wasn't about any of you. It was a piece about shopping in New York. I sold it to the Peridot Corporation and it's due to be published in their feminist magazine next month. Phone them if you don't believe me—which none of you ever does.'

She rounded on Calum. 'And yes, I looked in the safe—to get back my passport which Chris locked away there so that I had to stay with him. Even though you offered me sixty thousand dollars to leave Chris and never darken his door again,' she added, glancing at Chris to see if he knew, and finding from the way he stiffened that he didn't. But she went on, 'And yes, I read about your nasty little secrets: buying off Francesca's boyfriend, your mistress passing off your child as her husband's. And you have the nerve, the bare-faced nerve, to accuse *me* of being immoral!'

'The article was on the computer,' Chris said rather hoarsely.

'And that's the only place. I wrote that to let off steam, but I had no intention of ever selling it. I would have wiped it off if I'd had time.' Her head came up. 'Contrary to your opinion of me, I would never sell dirt like that to anyone, not even about you two hypocrites, especially when it involved innocent people. An innocent child who doesn't know he has a louse for a father!' she said venomously to Calum, who flushed, for once disconcerted.

'But you tried to blackmail me,' Francesca cut in. 'That day you came to the restaurant. You brought in Andy Sims' name.'

'So?'

'So why else would you mention him if it wasn't to get money out of me?'

Tiffany laughed. 'My God, your mind! I thought you might still be in love with him. I thought your marriage might have broken down because of that. I went to tell you that he hadn't deserted you, but that you had been forced apart by your conniving, interfering cousin. I was going to tell you how you could find him. I'd found out his telephone number in California and had it all ready to give to you.' Tiffany gave her a derisive look. 'But you didn't even remember his name!'

Francesca flushed and went to speak, but Calum cut in, 'The fact remains that the documents are still missing from the safe. You might not have had a chance to sell them or the article.'

Tiffany laughed incredulously. 'If I were all the things you accuse me of, if all I wanted was money, I'd have used those papers to blackmail you, wouldn't I? And again, if all I'd wanted was money I'd have put the pressure on you to give me more to leave Chris—especially when I found I was pregnant.'

Francesca gasped and Calum stared at her. 'You're pregnant? You're sure?'

From behind her Chris said heavily, 'She had an abortion.'

Tiffany's chin came up. 'Which rather proves that I don't want your money. All I ever wanted was the sum Chris had promised me.' She turned to give him a withering glance. 'Which I'd more than earned.'

There was silence for a moment, but then Calum said insistently, 'The papers are still missing. You've brought them here with you and we want them back. Where are they?'

Tiffany gave him a disparaging look. 'Chris did my packing for me; ask him if he put them in my case. And he emptied everything out of my bag that day. Ask him if your terribly important documents were in it.'

'No,' Chris admitted. He was watching her closely, conflicting emotions in his eyes.

'So where are they?' Calum demanded.

'In the flat in New York, of course. In one of the kitchen drawers.' She looked at Chris. 'You must have left New York very soon after me, because you'll also find a letter waiting for you there that I mailed after I left, telling you where to find the papers.' She paused and added, 'It also contains a cheque for the extra money you gave me. I never wanted more than you'd promised.' Chris made a gesture towards her but she went on quickly, 'The letter also says that what happened to Calum and Francesca in their past is purely their own concern and nothing to do with me. Everyone makes mistakes; no one should have to live with them forever.'

His gaze was on her and she looked at him steadily as she spoke. Both of them had forgotten the others as he frowned, shook his head and said, 'There are some things that are unforgivable.'

'Yes, there are,' she agreed. 'Unforgivable things have been done to me—that's why I could never——'

She broke off. Isabel had discovered that she was locked in and was rattling the bedroom door-handle angrily and shouting to be let out.

Calum took the key from his pocket, but said, 'If I find that you've been lying and that article appears...'

'It won't,' Tiffany said shortly.

'Do you really expect us to believe that?'

'I do,' Francesca said unexpectedly. 'And in a way I'm grateful to Tiffany for bringing this out into the open; I'd always wondered why Andy took off so suddenly and never wrote. It changed me, made me uncertain about myself, but I pretended to be very sophisticated to compensate. It made me get my values wrong for a very long time.' She looked at Tiffany, her eyes vulnerable. 'I did remember him, that day in New York, but I didn't want you to know how much he had mattered.'

Tiffany looked at her in surprise, wondering what could possibly have brought about such a change. But with a flash of feminine insight she realised that Francesca hadn't really changed at all, that basically she was much like herself, hurting inside but showing only a hard outer shell to the world. Well, Tiffany knew all about shells and walls; only Francesca's shell had been so diamond-encrusted that it had taken her own admission for Tiffany to see that the glittering sophistication had been only a brittle defence.

She was beginning to think that maybe she and Francesca could have been friends after all, when Chris touched her arm and said, 'What were you going to say?'

Isabel was banging and kicking the door and Calum went quickly to let her out. She shot out of the bedroom, yelling her anger in Portuguese, and it was a few minutes before Tiffany could quiet her.

'It's all right; everything is fine. Come on, we're going now.'

'No. Wait.'

Chris tried to take her arm but Isabel glared at him angrily. 'You leave Tiffany alone, you. You got her thrown out of the boarding house into the street. You knew she had no money so she was forced to go with you, live with you. We wanted to help her but she has too much pride. She would rather sell herself to a pig like you than take from her friends.'

'But you're wrong. I——'

'It wasn't Chris.' Francesca's voice broke in on them. Her face pale, she said, 'It was me. I told the landlord she was there. I was angry that she'd gatecrashed the party. And I was afraid that Calum was falling for her. I followed them when he took her home, found out where she was staying. It was perfectly obvious she wasn't supposed to be there from the way the key was thrown down to her, so I knew that she'd lied and was trying to trick us—trick Calum. So the next day I checked with the landlord and—and told him.' She gave Tiffany a pained look. 'I'm sorry. I didn't know how desperate you were.'

Tiffany shrugged. 'It really doesn't matter.' Then she gave a small laugh. 'It must have been quite a shock for you to find that you'd turned Calum against me, only to have Chris—make use of me instead.'

'It was never that,' Chris said harshly.

'No? Well, that doesn't matter either.' She lifted a hand to push her hair back from her face, the loose shirt she was wearing over her trousers riding up a little. 'I really think that's everything. Come on, Isabel, let's go.'

But Chris moved in front of her. 'I must speak to you, alone.'

Tiffany looked at him for a moment, at the features she had grown to love and had missed so unbearably since he'd thrown her out. But today he had accused her of the most despicable things, so she shook her head. 'There's nothing left to say.'

Quickly she turned and hurried out of the flat, Isabel close behind her, protecting her when Chris reached out to stop her. He looked as if he was going to pick Isabel up and move her bodily out of the way, but Calum caught his arm and pulled him back.

The corridors of the old monastery were long and tiled. Tiffany's footsteps echoed as she took fresh flowers up to the room of a nice Dutch couple who'd been staying there for several days. The hotel was very new, the people who owned it having spent a whole year and a great deal of money on transforming the monks' cells into five-star luxury bedrooms for guests, the refectory into a magnificent dining-room, the cloister courtyard into a beautiful garden with a central fountain. The work was still far from finished—there was still the outdoor pool and the gymnasium et cetera to be done—but enough rooms had been equipped with antique beds and furniture for them to open the hotel.

Tiffany enjoyed working and living here; there was the excitement of a new project, the occasional emergency and panic when things went wrong because they hadn't worked out a foolproof system yet. And the owners and staff were friendly, understanding. The hours were irregular; often she had to stay late at the front desk, seeing off departing diners, or waiting to let in late guests. But Tiffany didn't mind that because it gave her the opportunity to have a few hours off during the day. Then she would go for a walk in the countryside, sometimes up paths that led through row upon row of grapevines, tiers that reached the tops of the surrounding hills and disappeared over the crest to climb the next peak. More often, though, she would walk to a walled viewpoint that looked out over the river, the Douro, which nestled in the valley below the monastery on its way downstream where it would pass the *palácio*, and the Brodey wine cellars, on its way to the sea. Then her thoughts were always full of what might have been if the world had been as perfect as a dream.

She was there now, the day after her visit to Oporto to see the *barco rabelo* race with Isabel. A day that had ended her connection with the Brodey family so finally. It needn't have done, she supposed; Chris had still wanted to talk to her, and she could have told him the truth. But what was the point? He had accused her of selling his family's secrets. Well, maybe he'd had reason enough, she thought, trying to be fair, but he had never given her the benefit of the doubt; none of the Brodeys had ever thought she was more than a gold-digger. Chris had never trusted her, not even enough to tell her he cared, not until that last day when he had thrown her out, and then it had been too late. And he had certainly never intended to marry her. Not, at least, until he'd known she was pregnant. But what kind of marriage would it have been, either then or now, when he could so easily believe the worst of her?

The breeze stirred her hair and she looked up at the sky. It was autumn now, the deep heat of summer gone and leaving a pleasant mildness in its place. The grape harvest had been gathered in and was fermenting in the great tanks in the *quintas*, the first stage in the port-wine-making process.

Behind her she heard a footstep and glanced round in surprise, then became very still as Chris climbed the path to join her. He came quickly, almost as if he was afraid she would run away from him, and his breathing was a little uneven as he stood before her.

For a moment she couldn't speak, then said, 'How did you find me?' in a voice she didn't recognise as her own.

'I went to the boarding house and found Isabel, made her tell me.' His eyes searched her face, then he said harshly, 'Tell me the truth. Did you have an abortion or not?'

She didn't try to prevaricate, just said with a sigh, 'I told you what I thought you wanted to hear. But when I found I was wrong you had got so angry you wouldn't listen to me.'

'You're still having it? You're still having the baby?'

'Yes, of course.'

'But why? I don't understand.'

Sadness came into her eyes. 'Of course you don't. Why should you? Right from the first you've always believed the worst of me: gold-digger, tramp. You even thought I'd got pregnant just to trap you into marriage. Why should I be surprised when you can't understand that I could never have had an abortion?' She turned her head away angrily. 'I don't know why the hell you came here. Just go away.'

'No! Never!' There was such positiveness in his tone that she turned again to look at him. Although his face was still bleak, there was a fierce determination in Chris's eyes, in the thrust of his chin. 'I'm not going to let you run out on me again,' he said shortly. 'I'm going to look after you and the child, care for you both whether you like it or not. And we're going to talk. There aren't going to be any more misunderstandings.'

He squared his shoulders, as if already taking on the responsibility for them all, and the playboy image that Tiffany had of him faded from her mind. Hope again fluttered in her heart but the emotion was so alien to her that she couldn't let it in, even had to try and push it away by saying stiffly, 'I appreciate your offer but I have a job, I can take care of myself. If you want to help—later, when the baby is born... But—but I don't need you.'

'Don't you?' His eyes met hers, searching into her soul.

'No.' She turned away again, unable to look him in the eye as she lied to him.

She heard him move closer, felt the lightest of touches on her hair. 'But *I* need *you!*' he suddenly said fiercely, and, catching hold of her, he made her face him. 'I love you and I can't live without you. Do you know what these last weeks have been like, trying to hate you for what I thought you'd done, and yet all the time wanting you, needing you, missing you? So much that every day without you was a living hell! I've been torn apart, trying to fight my feelings for you, telling myself you were no good, and yet all the time there was a basic instinct that wouldn't let me believe you were evil, that wouldn't stop loving you. That article was only an excuse; I would have gone on looking for you for as long as it took.' His grip tightened, his face tense with trying to make her understand.

Tiffany stared up at him, unable to speak, unable to feel anything but the wild, unfamiliar happiness that was starting to grow in her heart.

But Chris took her silence for denial. Letting her go, he looked out over the river and said bleakly, 'I can understand that after what's happened between us you won't want to be with me, but I won't let your pride stop me from helping you, and I won't let you shut me out of your life.'

Looking at his set profile, Tiffany gathered her courage and placed her whole life and that of her child in his hands as she said slowly, 'Not having an abortion wasn't just a matter of—of principle. There was another reason.' He swung swiftly round to look at her and she raised a strained face to his. 'How could I possibly have destroyed the only part of you that was really mine?'

Chris's eyes widened incredulously; he reached out an unsteady hand and put it on her shoulder. 'Tiffany, what—what are you saying?'

She bit her lip and it was a moment before she could go on. 'I tried so hard to hate you. I thought that you were intrigued because I didn't fawn all over you. I thought it amused you to use me. I thought you were like all the others.'

She expected him to question her then, but instead he said simply, 'I was attracted to you the first time I saw you, deeply attracted. It hurt like hell when I thought you were making a play for Calum. Afterwards, when you agreed to come to me, you seemed so antagonistic.' His trembling hand stroked her cheek. 'I think I fell in love with you right from the start, but I was afraid to let you see it. I hoped that if I kept you with me long enough you might come to feel the way I did, but then everything seemed to go so horribly wrong.'

Tiffany gave a shaky laugh. 'It was my fault. It took me so long to realise how I felt about you.' She raised pleading eyes to his. 'I'm not very good at—at love.'

Putting his arm round her, Chris held her against him. 'Tell me,' he said simply.

'It's hard. I've never told anyone before. Does it—does it matter?'

'No. I thought I'd lost you and I knew that my life was nothing without you. I found that out as soon as you'd gone. I was so angry with you, and yet I missed you unbearably. And I was furious when I found that article on the computer, but I seized the excuse it gave me to find you. I know now that nothing matters so long as we're together.' A smile lit his eyes. 'The three of us.'

'Oh, Chris.' She buried her head against his shoulder and for a few moments he held her very tightly, but then she moved away a little and said, 'My childhood was wonderfully happy until I was twelve. Then my mother got multiple sclerosis. Before that she'd been very fit, taken part in lots of sports and activities. It devastated her—and my father. He tried but he couldn't take it. He walked out. I was an only child, and I had to look after her; there was no one else.'

She paused, then, her voice becoming expressionless, she went on, 'Because—because of these terrible things happening to her my mother—went a little crazy. People with MS get remission periods. Whenever my mother felt better she would take a lover, have him move in with us. It was as if she had to prove to herself that she was still attractive to men. My father had given her the house, but one of the men, when she became ill again, persuaded her to borrow money against it. He took most of it. We had to move into a flat.'

She paused but Chris said nothing, sensing that she needed to gather her courage to go on. 'When I got older, my mother was weaker, even in her good periods. She had to rest a lot and I left school early to stay home and look after her. It was impossible for me to get a job, train for a career. Then one of her men tried to seduce me. When I complained to my mother she blamed me and sent me away to France to pick grapes. I was too young to move out and my father wouldn't help; he had married again and he didn't answer my letters—if he ever got them. There were other men: towards the end my mother would pick up anyone she could get. They took every penny she had. One of them threatened to hurt my mother if I didn't...'

She stopped, unable to go on, and Chris pulled her to him and held her close again. 'Oh, my darling girl, it's all right. It's all right. Don't go on. You're safe now.'

For a while she stood in the comfort of his arms, but then lifted pain-filled eyes to say, 'My mother's doctor helped me. He got her into a hospital, but she had been ill for so long, took so long to die. Years of physical and mental torment, of being used and mistreated by men. I hated men after that, hated all of them. It took me a long while even to begin to think that you could be different.'

His arms still circling her, his eyes holding hers, Chris said, 'But now?'

'But now I know I love you,' she said simply. 'So maybe our baby was conceived in love after all.'

Chris bent to kiss her, lovingly, lingeringly. Straightening, he smiled, a smile of the deepest happiness, and let her go to take her hand. 'Come on, we've got lots to do.'

'We have?'

Helping her down the path with great care, he said, 'Yes, we've got to get back to Oporto right away.'

'But my job...'

'I'm afraid you'll have to give it up. You'll have far more important things to do.'

'What things?'

'Preparing for our wedding, of course.'

Tiffany stood still and stared at him. '*What* did you say?'

'We'll have it exactly the way you wanted it, the way you described it to that woman in America—in Oporto Cathedral. And we'll have Francesca as bridesmaid.'

She was still staring at him. 'Chris, you can't mean it.'

'Of course I mean it.'

'But what about your family? Calum? Your parents?'

'I'm marrying you, not them. And anyway, when they know you they'll all love you as much as I do. So I intend to marry you with as much ceremony as I can contrive.'

'I'd be happy in just a register office so long as it was with you.'

His eyes filled with love, but Chris said, 'You seem to forget you're marrying a Brodey. It's going to be a magnificent wedding.' He grinned. 'Perhaps slightly hurried, but definitely magnificent.'

Tiffany looked at him, then said huskily, 'Come here.'

He raised an eyebrow, but came to stand in front of her.

'There's something I want to do.' And for the first time in her life, for the first time with this man she was to marry, Tiffany reached up to give a kiss that she wanted to give, and gave it with all the love, thankfulness and happiness in her heart.

Coming Next Month

HARLEQUIN PRESENTS®

THE BEST HAS JUST GOTTEN BETTER

#1833 THE FATHER OF HER CHILD Emma Darcy
Lauren didn't want to fall in love again—but when she saw Michael all her good resolutions went out the window. And when she learned he was out to break her heart she vowed never to see him again. But it was too late....

#1834 WILD HUNGER Charlotte Lamb
Book Four: *SINS*
Why was Gerard, famous foreign correspondent, following Keira? She could hardly believe he was interested in the story of a supermodel fighting a constant battle with food. No, he wanted something more....

#1835 THE TROPHY HUSBAND Lynne Graham
(9 to 5)
When Sara caught her fiancé being unfaithful, her boss, Alex, helped pick up the pieces of her life. But Sara wondered what price she would have to pay for his unprecedented kindness.

#1836 THE STRENGTH OF DESIRE Alison Fraser
(This Time, Forever)
The death of Hope's husband brought his brother, Guy, back into her life, and left her with two legacies. Both meant that neither Hope nor Guy would be able to forget their erstwhile short-lived affair.

#1837 FRANCESCA Sally Wentworth
(Ties of Passion, 2)
Francesca was used to having the best of everything—and that included men. The uncouth Sam was a far cry from her usual boyfriends, but he was the only man who had ever loved her for what she was rather than what she had.

#1838 TERMS OF POSSESSION Elizabeth Power
Nadine needed money—and Cameron needed a child. His offer was extraordinary—he would possess her body and soul and the resulting baby would be his. But the arrangements were becoming complicated...

HARLEQUIN PRESENTS®

THIS TIME, FOREVER

THE PAST
Guy had once been the only man
Hope could turn to.

THE PRESENT
Now he was back!

THE FUTURE
And once again Jack's behavior was
pushing Hope into Guy's arms.
Would this time be forever?

Watch for:
#1836 THE STRENGTH OF DESIRE
by Alison Fraser

Available in September wherever
Harlequin books are sold.

Look us up on-line at: http://www.romance.net

TTF3